The

Broken Vessel

Don't be a victim;

be a vessel.

By Tosha Suggs

I humbly dedicate this book to my mother, Mary B. Suggs.

My vision came light in your absence, gone but never forgotten.

Acknowledgments

I want to thank my son, Christopher, for always being light on dark days. You are my favorite part of life. Also, to my TRUE family and friends (there's a difference), thank you for understanding me and having patience. Lastly," The Book Doctor," for seeing my first book as a vessel to everyone who reads it. I personally want to thank Shav'ae (Zen) Johnson for the book cover illustration. She's an upcoming artist currently attending SCAD in Savannah, GA. May God continue to bless your artistic journey.

Charlie

All happy families are alike. They all grow up together eating at the table, and no one fights, no one says anything mean towards the other, but unhappy families, that's a different case.

Her name was Charlotte, but everyone called her Charlie. Despite her confined life, Charlie was a free-spirited soul. She was a little girl who wanted to love life, but it felt like life did not love her so many times. Scattered and fractured as it is, this is her story.

Charlie's world was consumed by brokenness: the broken commitment by her biological father who abandoned her when she was a baby, the fragmented care of her useless mother who chose to put her desires for a man over her responsibility to her daughter, and a family who criticized her for being the result of the hurt and pain they created.

The other night Charlie got a call from an old friend who wanted to unearth old wounds instead of healing them. This night was no different from any other night in vivacious Tampa, Florida. It was the dead of winter, and she could hear the wind howling outside her door. Having a house on the beach has its advantages. You can smell the night air and feel the wind across your body. It's usually relaxing, but on a night like this, you can almost feel the storm approaching. The palm trees beat against the windows with the warning that something was coming.

This made Charlie think of all of the storms she had faced that brought her to this current place. The storms of raging hate, anger, resentment, and neglect that yielded to freedom. She pulled the terrycloth robe closer to her and walked over to the front door to make sure she locked it. Funny, she would do that sometimes. Satisfied that she was sufficiently safe, she checked on Grace. Then, she glanced over at the etagere and spotted the tattered vase that her mother gave her. Well, she didn't actually give it to her.

Charlie took it the day she left. It was the only thing she wanted out of that hopeless home, if you could even call it a home.

This vase made her smile and cry simultaneously. She could still see the cracks on the left side when her mom dropped it during one of her fits with Clint. Charlie glued it back together as best she could, but the damage was still there. The cracks in the vessel mirrored Charlie's life. But now, back to her childhood.

Charlie grew up in Durham, North Carolina, in a single-parent household. She and her mom, Dorothy, lived in a dead and dreary apartment in the dirtiest parts of North Carolina. The stench of the place would make you gag. The Hood was what most people called it.

This was during a time when Blacks were just identifying themselves and families were making the most of what they had, which was nothing. It was the late 70's, and the music of Motown filled the air in many homes, hoping for change. You could hear Marvin Gaye asking what's going on and the melodic voice of Stevie Wonder whispering in your ear.

Charlie was no stranger to the kids in the neighborhood. She spent her weekends with a nanny who lived across the street and verbally and mentally abused her. Mrs. Elaine was the neighborhood Grinch and the cheapest babysitter in town. Her apartment was cold, wet, and lifeless. It always had an eerie feeling with the aroma of rubbing alcohol and bergamot hair grease.

Dorothy was a hard-worker, yet she was troubled. It was difficult for her to deal with past trauma and abuse and manage raising a child from a broken vessel.

Dorothy never publicly acknowledged it, but her movements and actions expressed that she never really wanted a child. Charlie was born into resentment and hostility, oftentimes enduring the aftermath of her mother's unaddressed issues.

But Dorothy was a modern-day hustler. She would work every day of the week as a cashier for a local mom-and-pop shop that sold tools and mechanical parts, although everyone in the neighborhood knew they were selling much more than basic tools. If you went around to the side door, you could get some liquid and powdered tools to help you cope with the world around you. However fortunate or unfortunate, Dorothy was not privy to the illegal dealings of the store. As a matter of fact, she didn't make much money, yet what she made kept up the section 8 payments and utilities.

She was not much of the Betty Crocker homemaker either. Cooking only consisted of eggs and toast, if that. Charlie's meals, which came from Ronald McDonald, were happy meals or any food the neighbors would provide for her. And when Dorothy did go grocery-shopping, she would purposely buy dented cans and demand a discount for the damaged cans she selected.

Dorothy never, ever bought any kind of treats or lovely things for Charlie. No cookies or even a birthday cake on her birthday. She didn't even make excuses for not buying them, but she could afford cigarettes and Valium. Go figure.

Poor thing, Charlie was severely malnourished and frail. This little girl never knew what it was like to be caressed or touched by a mother who naturally cared for her. Dorothy thought working all the time was the right thing for them. Work was an escape for Dorothy to avoid the responsibility of rearing her child in the right direction.

Their daily routine wasn't the typical peaches and roses like most households. The reoccurring conversations would consist of Dorothy belittling Charlie.

"Charlie, get your lazy, ugly self up for school and do something with that tired, matted-up hair you got."

"Yes, ma'am," she'd say, retreating to her room silently crying, feeling the truth in the lies her mom spewed at her.

These verbally abusive conversations encompassed their daily bonding, not much positive affirmation. You would think they were strangers co-existing just enough to make it through the dreadful mornings.

Although Charlie was clothed, her mom would only shop at the stores in the neighborhood that were known for having poor quality clothing. The clothes weren't ugly, but they never fit right. Sometimes one sleeve was longer than the other, or the hem was ripped in different places. The sizes were rarely accurate. A small was actually a medium, and a medium was actually a large. Charlie got used to her clothes being either too big or too small. Eventually she also got used to being picked on for her ill-fitting garments.

Dorothy failed at most of the essential functions of mothering: nurturing, helping her child grow up and become independent and foster a secure sense of identity. Rather than encourage, she would frequently tongue-lash the young girl over everything she did. To cope, Charlie would cry her tears into her favorite blue vase. She never had the opportunity to know how to have conversations or how to express herself with anyone. She was always alone, heartbroken, and crying most of the time.

Who would even want to play with her? Her matted hair alone was enough to make any parent snatch away a child who started to befriend Charlie. Even if she tried to make friends, she couldn't talk to them. Her companions were the deep, scary thoughts she had created in her mind for a very long time.

The agony of their week usually ended as Friday came. Dorothy found yet another way to disconnect herself. On the weekends, she would transform into another person, an attention seeker, gold-digger, and a narcissist.

That new Dorothy would leave on Friday evening and return on Sunday night. She worked the nightclubs on weekends, entertaining menfolk or anyone with the highest dollar amount. Charlie slowly morphed into a victim of a broken vessel, routinely packing her dirty rags to be left with Mrs. Elaine.

One would never know Mrs. Elaine was the reason for some of Charlie's trauma as well as several other kid's trauma. She was the Dr. Jekyll and Mr. Hyde to the kids she fostered and cared for. The little darlings were subject to belittling and an appalling lack of food. She took full advantage of parents who desperately needed someone to watch their children while they worked. She manipulated the parents into thinking she was feeding their kids sumptuous, home-cooked meals and providing exceptional care. And of course, it worked.

Who would not believe it when she welcomes you with beaming smiles and talks gently to the children, carrying them on her hips as if she loved them.

Unsuspecting moms and dads could smell the grease popping from the fried chicken drying out on paper napkins. Warm peach cobbler fresh out of the oven competed for your nostril's attention with baked macaroni and farm-picked snap peas coming in a close second and third place. When these aromas filled the air, you just knew your child was about to eat good. But you would have been dead wrong.

That food was only for Mrs. Elaine. She kept several old containers of cheese and crackers for her young prisoners. If they were extra helpful, they got a lukewarm juice box. Many of the children would be subject to isolation if they did not follow her rules.

However, on the outside, she was the perfect visionary to those who didn't really know her. They saw her as a kind, wonderful woman who cared for children. Parents loved her because they thought she had a gentle spirit. They didn't pay attention to the children's cries and pleas when it was time for them to go there. The kids saw the demonic spirit Mrs. Elaine really was, but they were threatened not to say anything for fear of being attacked when they returned to her home.

Charlie endured the abuse every weekend. For some reason, Mrs. Elaine treated Charlie different from the other kids. Perhaps she sensed Charlie's timidity and low self-confidence and wanted to exploit them as much as possible.

The other kids had some leeway. They did the dusting, mopping, and ironing. They had a few opportunities to eat the meager food and play with the broken toys after their chores were done, but not Charlie. She would sit in the filth of food and mud that had been thrown at her by Mrs. Elaine. Charlie's chores would be scrubbing the floors with the toothbrush she brought from home or scrubbing the callouses off the bottom of Mrs. Elaine's feet.

Over the weekend, Charlie didn't bathe. She would often urinate on herself to keep from going to the bathroom because she feared that Mrs. Elaine would lock the door from the outside. She actually did that once.

If Charlie protested in any way, she would get the worst beating of her life. That is one thing Dorothy never did, beat Charlie. I guess Mrs. Elaine took care of that for her.

Charlie did not have anyone to tell the bitter details of the abuse. Her mom could care less because she was so wrapped up in her own life, trying as much as possible to exclude her unwanted daughter. Charlie did not matter; she didn't want her at all. The sight of the frail, little girl made Dorothy sad and regretful.

When her weekend work was done, Dorothy would gather her belongings, meaning Charlie, on Sunday evening to start the weekly drama all over again. Charlie was Dorothy's luggage, the baggage she carried around from one place to the next.

This lasted for about two years. Charlie was drowning deeper in self-pity and her tears. That trauma was too much for a little kid. How could her mother not even have a soft spot for her, even if just a teeny weeny one? But no, not

Dorothy. She never bothered to care about Charlie, and Charlie knew it.

They say when a storm is approaching, you know it. Perhaps you have to be a certain age for this awareness to take effect because Charlie never saw this tornado coming.

One minute she and Dorothy were living their mundane, roommate lifestyle, and the next thing you know a third person interrupts the existence of the odd couple.

A strange, shabby-looking man showed up with the same luggage her mom carried around. This strange man was one of many men who accompanied Dorothy. She would have many visitors during the week, and they would engage in everything from drugs to loud sex as though there wasn't a young child in the house.

Although many men came around, this man was the only one who actually moved into their tiny, Section 8 residence. The home seemed to become a tad bit brighter when he showed up. He would soon be the provider for Charlie and her part-time step father/mother.

His name was Clint, a well-spoken gentleman with eyes of hope and promise. He came in as a king, ready to rule his castle. He had no clue that Dorothy was certainly no queen, but more like the wicked witch of the palace.

Clint got the hint really quick though. During the week, Clint would take care of Charlie, who spent most of her nights hidden in her room. Regrettably, she still went with Mrs. Elaine on the weekends; nothing changed there until Mrs. Elaine got sick and could not babysit anymore. Small mercies.

Some said Mrs. Elaine went away because one of the parents reported her for child neglect; of course, that was a rumor.

So Clint became the full-time provider, weekdays and weekends, while Charlie was sinking further into depression at the age of six. Clint was never there for the extra responsibilities, but looking at Charlie, frail and dry, he stepped in at the right time.

Then Clint's baggage popped up in the middle of the night with bags in hand. Corey and his two sisters entered the scene full of sadness and became a part of that cracked vase, the vessels that Charlie never needed.

When the three musketeers arrived, things got even worse for Charlie. They were all older than Charlie. The oldest sister, Roxy, hated Charlie, and she was actually the QUEEN of the castle. Corey was a disturbed young boy who was controlled by Roxy. It was always Corey, do this;

Corey, do that. The baby girl, Jean, was mentally incapable of caring for herself or anyone else. She was born a preemie, addicted to crack, so she functioned like a five-year-old even though she was 10.

Clint had moved from New York to North Carolina, far away from the daily drug-addicted wife and disrespectful kids. Now, he was forced to take the responsibility of four torn children while Dorothy hid from the fragmented family by working as much as she could.

Charlie could not imagine the hurt she was about to face from her new mother, Roxy, who became the caretaker for all of the kids.

Clint only stepped in when things did not go his way. Clint ran a military camp, and he trained Roxy to be his commander-in-charge. He thought his military discipline would give us the best direction.

After his stint in the Marines as a mechanic, he realized that life is hard and unfair. After he retired, he met the love of his life. She was captivating with chocolate skin as soft as a baby's bottom. He was blown away from the first day, imagining a life of endless possibilities with Carol.

At first, everything was lovely. They started a family right away, and were content with living in their tiny but warm apartment. When Roxy was still a toddler, Corey came along. That was when Carol began acting strange. Perhaps she thought motherhood would be different. Although she liked the idea of being pregnant, she seemed to be experiencing postpartum depression well after the kids were born. A friend introduced her to crack to help her cope, and it was all downhill from there.

Clint was so focused on taking care of Corey and Roxy that he didn't realize what was going on with Carol. By the time Jean was born, Carol had stopped trying to hide her habit. Clint tried to stay, but he could not take the embarrassment of having an addict for a wife.

Roxy carried so much bitterness. She remembered what it was like before her mom became an addict and resented her dad for leaving when the family needed him the most.

At home in North Carolina, Roxy was like the mother and wife; she took on the cooking and cleaning, but she was deeply damaged. The young girl who had to grow up too soon took her hatred out on the most likely target. Roxy would sexually abuse Charlie while everyone was asleep or busy with chores. Soon, Roxy would make Corey touch Charlie as well. He hated those moments. The brother and sister duo would hold Charlie down and run their fingers through her virgin body. Charlie's mouth would be covered, her arms pinned to the floor, and her legs tied together. There was nowhere for her to go or shout out for help. Her life was a living Stephen King movie, a life no one would ever wish for.

Roxy enjoyed torturing Charlie. You could see the gleam in her eyes when she touched Charlie's body.

After a few weeks of being in Durham, Roxy became close friends with the neighbors next door; it was a family that had three boys. The most unfavorable three boys anyone could ask for: Reggie, Curt, and Jamie. Reggie and Curt were the boys everyone was afraid of, but not Roxy. She was aroused by them. Their match-up was indescribable, a match of devilish and sinister-minded youth who were always up for mischief.

Roxy told Reggie and Curt about the excitement with Charlie. They loved hearing about the way Roxy handled Charlie. Their beady eyes were filled with eagerness when Roxy told them of the pleasure she had with Charlie. They wanted to make Charlie their sexual puppet too. Because Jamie was too young to understand what they were doing, he just followed along with his brothers. He was charged with the task of pinning Charlie's feeble body down while Roxy, Reggie and Curt caressed Charlie's forbidden fruit.

Clint and Dorothy were clueless about Charlie and the abuse. Clint was more worried about Dorothy's weekend escapades. She would leave on Friday afternoon and come back Saturday morning. Sadly, he didn't know the real evil that was brewing in his own home.

Charlie began to withdraw more and more from the world around her in a sea of depression. At this point, Charlie could not be saved, and no one was there who cared. In their small, Section 8 home, the abuse and neglect went on for two years until Charlie was eight years old.

Eventually, Clint decided to move them to another home, far from the dirty projects and into a nicer place in Charlotte. Dorothy was still absent and unbothered, leaving the stepdad as the sole provider for Charlie and the rest of the kids. Clint thought Dorothy would stay home more since he moved them into a better home and provided the meals and whatever else they needed. Little did he know that that was the only reason Dorothy was with him, but nothing he did made her behavior change.

Dorothy was tired of being broke, paying rent, and taking care of Charlie. She needed to use someone to take on her responsibility so she could live her life fully to herself. No matter where they moved, she would never love or truly want to be with Clint.

The new home was bigger and brighter. It smelled like the fresh breakfast Clint made in the mornings. The new smell of crispy bacon, fluffy eggs, and the kids' favorite, stewed potatoes. You could smell the aroma through the vibrantly painted walls.

The house was a dream come true with five bedrooms and three bathrooms: a fantasy. Who would've thought they all shared a small bathroom before and now had three bathrooms in a big house?

In the new house, the sexual abuse turned to torture. Roxy would lock Charlie in the closet if she did anything wrong or threatened to tell on her. As Roxy got older, she became more enraged with anger and bitterness, bitterness from a mother who died from a drug overdose and a dad who left them in their time of need. And she took all of it out on Charlie.

"How do you like that, idiot?"

"Please, Roxy…" Charlie whimpered.

"Spit my name out of your filthy mouth, you wench," Roxy slapped her hard.

To Roxy, Charlie was the one who ruined her family, and Roxy wanted the little wench to suffer, to feel pain until she couldn't anymore, and then give up.

When Roxy started to gain interest in boys, this helped Charlie a bit. Roxy began to leave Charlie alone as her relationships grew with the local boys. Roxy never apologized to Charlie, nor did she acknowledged the hurt she caused. She acted like she was right, like Charlie deserved the harsh treatment.

The trauma lingered until Dorothy and Clint went their separate ways. Clint was sick and tired of Dorothy.

"This is over, Dorothy," he said to her as he stood by the door. Charlie sat quietly in a dark corner, not moving and watching what was going on.

"What do you mean?"

"I'm tired of all this. You don't do anything! It's hard to even get to see you in a day. You're always going here and there. I regret ever moving in with you," Clint said angrily.

"Excuse me!" Dorothy put her lipstick down and turned to look at Clint.

"It's over between us, I've had enough of your nonsense, and I can't go on like this anymore."

"But Clint, there is nothing wrong with how we live or how often I'm here. You are just getting worked up over nothing," she said nonchalantly. "I told you before we got together that I wasn't going to be a puppy you could order around with housework, and you agreed. You understood, right?"

"No, I thought I could, but I don't seem to understand you. You don't play your role as a mother and a girlfriend. What good woman leaves her home uncared for and roams the streets? You, Dorothy, are not a good woman for my kids, and I am done with you."

"You can't do this to me, Clint!" He was throwing her out with nowhere else to go. She had no money and nobody to help.

"Fine! I'm leaving, Clint, and I know you are going to regret this! There are better men out there than you. All you did was confine me!"

"Just leave!" He left the door open as she angrily stormed past him.

The bags of clothes were already piled at the door. Clint was done with Dorothy. There was no union between them. There was not one day that she had stayed to take care of the home for even an hour or two. She was always in the streets, her life was the streets, and that was where she belonged. He pitied poor Charlie, but she wasn't his child, and he didn't want to take her from her mom.

Clint went on to find another woman who would continue the pattern of taking his kindness for weakness, using him to keep a roof over her head while doing whatever she wanted on the side. He did try, poor thing, but he never took the time to be alone and care for his children. He just had to have a woman around.

When Roxy was old enough to move out, she followed down her mother's path with having child after child after child. She didn't develop a crack habit, but she did end up doing time in prison.

Working 12 hours at a time a coming home to basically sleep and eat, she left Jean home to care for the three children. Roxy had taught Jean how to change pampers and feed the children. Aside from those two tasks, they just watched television and played with toys.

For a while, things seemed to be going well, until Roxy came home to find Jean fisting her five-year-old daughter. Roxy lost it and beat Jean until she was unconscious.

Jean lie half naked on the kitchen floor, her blood coloring the dusty tile. Roxy sat at the kitchen table without moving for three days. Three whole days. She didn't bathe. She didn't eat. She didn't call the police to tell them what she did or what her dead sister had done. She just sat there. Not even aroused by the screams and cries from her children who'd begun to taste the blood that painted the floor.

On the third day, the police walked into the unlocked house to find the scene after the neighbors complained about the children's incessant screams. Roxy was charged with voluntary manslaughter, cruelty to children, and oddly enough, child sexual abuse. The five-year-old told the cops, "She hurt me," and they assumed the child was referring to Roxy who said nothing to defend herself. Perhaps turnabout is fair play.

Corey rescued his three nieces so they would not be wards of the state, but he was still a young man himself. Clint agreed to raise the girls so Corey could attend college and try to make a better life for himself.

Charlie and Dorothy moved to a small duplex where Charlie was left to take care of herself. Dorothy was still running the streets, more than before, and Charlie would spend many days and nights alone, mindlessly drowning in loneliness.

It was as if she was back at Mrs. Elaine's house. Dorothy treated her like a slave, demanding Charlie to cook and clean. At the same time, she partied or disappeared for weekends and sometimes weeks at a time. Charlie was repeatedly told how dumb and stupid she was. Nothing the young girl did was acceptable, and she could not talk to her mom. Even if she did try, Dorothy would never listen. They were simply two strangers cohabitating together.

It's natural to assume that if Charlie was born into a different family or perhaps had a different mother that she would have had a much better childhood. Would having a mother who was emotionally strong make circumstances more favorable? Having someone who could tell her each day that she was worth it or just assure her that she believed in her would have made a world of difference. Or would it?

In the game of life, we don't always get the cards we want; we are forced to play the cards we're dealt. You check your hand, hope for a joker or a spade, but if you don't get them, you use what you have. The interesting thing is that despite your knowledge of the deck, you have no idea what cards are in other players' hands. And how they play their hand often affects how you play yours.

In order to understand the why of Charlie's life, we have to first look at the hand her mother was dealt and how she played it.

Dorothy

Dorothy was born into a two-parent household with four older brothers. The youngest three brothers were the big brothers from HELL. They were horrible bullies who terrorized their neighborhood just for the fun of it. They would fight each other constantly, oftentimes to the point where there would be blood or broken body parts. The triple threat would try to kill each other at home, at school they would team up to terrorize other kids. Hearing their names sent fear up and down the spines of the quiet kids who got good grades and had lunchboxes instead of paper bags. The site of the barbaric boys made some hide themselves in lockers or stand on top of bathroom stalls to try and outsmart the trio. But it usually didn't work.

Dorothy's dad, Sam, was a traveling salesman, so he was rarely home to keep control of the chaos. Her mom, a private nurse, would work overnight sometimes, so Dorothy's oldest brother, Raymond, took care of the cooking and cleaning. Although it wasn't easy to keep the trio in check, he managed to put things back in order after they ransacked the house.

Ray was much older than the other boys, who always thought he was not biologically their dad's child. But they never said this out loud. Dorothy remembered Ray as her provider and protector, the one who nurtured her into womanhood.

Sam saw the kids only once or twice a month. He wasn't much of a father or a dad. When he was home, he would argue with Dorothy's mom, Brenda. They would have full-blown screaming matches, and Raymond would have to take the kids away from the house.

"How bout we turn around to get some ice cream." Raymond maneuvered Dorothy in the opposite direction and smiled at the boys.

"But we just got back from the park. We're tired," the trio whined.

"I know…" Ray said calmly. "I promise you'll get your favorite flavors."

"You promise!?" Dorothy squealed in delight.

"I promise!" He smiled and carried her on his shoulders.

"Okay, okay."

"Ray, I want chocolate flavor, and vanilla too… and… and banana too," Dorothy sang happily as they walked.

Even from a distance, Ray could tell when a storm was brewing at the house. He would get this uneasy feeling, and then his ear would start to ache, the prelude to the screaming they would be met with if they continued to the house.

The trio had witnessed a few fights despite Raymonds efforts. He didn't want Dorothy to see the fights. He promised himself each day that she wasn't going to end up like her father and mother when she grew up.

Chaos would be going on inside the home, but when Brenda, Sam, and the kids went out in public, the family was casket sharp. No one ever knew how bad things were. In fact, the neighbors saw them as a quiet, easy-going family. To them, Brenda was always polite, and her husband was a hardworking businessman who traveled due to his work.

Dorothy did not realize the dysfunction until she was 10 years old, an experience she wished she could forget.

Raymond had stepped away from the house to restock the refrigerator, and he left Dorothy in his room playing with her doll baby. Sam had separated himself from Brenda, so the house had been much quieter for some time now.

With mischief in mind, Brenda called Sam over to the house. She told him that Dorothy was smelling herself with some boy from the neighborhood and that she caught her lifting up her skirt behind the bushes for the little boy to touch her juice box. Dorothy would never do anything like that, but that was the only thing that Brenda could think of to get Sam to come over.

He came over in an outrage, wanting to know where Dottie was. He was the only person who called Dorothy Dottie. Brenda couldn't stand it when he first came up with the nickname. It made her feel like he liked Dottie more, which was actually true.

Sam walked in and went straight to Dorothy's room. He barely said two words to Brenda. Upset and confused, he came back into the living room trying to figure out where the gal was at. He didn't think to look into any other room.

"Brenda, what's going on? Where is Dottie?"

"Calm down, Sugar. Come sit next to me on the couch so I can explain."

"I don't want to sit next to you. I want to know where Dottie is."

"She ain't here, Sam."

"What the hell do you mean 'she ain't here'?"

"I told a little white lie. She didn't actually do what I said she did. I wanted you to come over so I could talk to you about something else.

Brenda told Sam the real reason she asked him to come over, and he just looked at her. She couldn't tell if he was getting aroused or angry. When she tried to reach her hand into his pants, she got her answer. Sam grabbed Brenda's hand and slung her across the room so hard and so fast that her wig landed in one corner, and she landed in the other. Sam looked up and saw Dorothy watching and dashed out of the door.

As if she felt no pain at all, Brenda slowly lifted herself off the floor, stood up, and limped to the restroom to clean herself up. Dorothy was dumbfounded. She had so many questions. How could her mother not fight back?

"What are you doing? Why didn't you defend yourself, Momma?"

"No, sweetie, I can't do that. A woman must never raise her hand up against a man."

"But is a man allowed to do the same?"

"You don't understand, baby. Just don't worry about it."

"But Momma… you…."

"Dorothy, you wouldn't understand. Some things aren't worth the fight. Sometimes you deserve what happens to you." She dabbed some water on her face.

Dorothy was too shocked and scared to say anything else. Brenda, swollen-eyed and hurt carried on as if nothing happened. Usually, Dorothy was shielded from seeing the beatings her mom would take. Raymond tried to protect his sister as much as he could, but nothing hindered her experience that day.

Dorothy was confused by what she saw and asked Raymond why their mom and dad were fighting this way.

"Raymond…" she said to him as he sat next to her.

"Yes, Dorothy."

"Would you ever beat the woman you love?"

"No."

"Would you make her feel sad all the time?"

"No."

"Do you think it's right to hit a woman?"

"No, it is not."

"What would you do to punish a woman if she hurt you?"

"I would tell her what she had done and tell her I don't like it."

"But you would never hit her, right?"

"Right, I wouldn't. Why are you asking me all these questions, Dorothy?"

"I saw dad hit mom today. He flung her across the room as if she was a piece of paper."

"You did, huh?" He was regretting leaving her at home.

"I asked mom why she didn't fight back, but she said it's not right for a woman to fight a man back. But is it right for a man to hit a woman?"

"No, it's not, Dorothy."

"Why did mom not fight back?"

"You wouldn't understand, Dorothy. You're still young, but I want you to know that no man will ever raise his hands to hit you."

"Will you hit me if I make you mad, Raymond?"

"I would never hit you or let anyone else hit you either." He pulled her close and patted her head.

Dorothy was left afraid of her dad, disappointed with her mom, and unsure of herself.

The one main motivator in her life took a beating and did nothing. Is that how a man expresses himself? If so, she knew she did not want a man. Dorothy's vision of herself and her mom changed forever that day.

Life went on as normal as possible. The brothers still carried on like a bunch of wild bulls. Raymond would try to break them up, but that only worsened matters. The fights would be over anything from school clothes they shared to the food they stole from the local deli. You name it; they would fight about it.

Brenda did her best to be there for Dorothy, but bitterness made Brenda avoid Dorothy at times. The young girl always looked decent, but she and her mom never had a real bond after that fatal fight. Brenda couldn't heal her own brokenness, so even looking at Dorothy each day made her sad. Brenda was a battered woman with deep scars. She did what she saw her mother do, and prayed that

Dorothy wouldn't follow in her footsteps, but she knew those prayers were in vain.

Even though Dorothy didn't have the mom she needed, she did have Raymond. He took Dorothy as a daughter rather than a sister, even walking her to school or arranging for the older girls to walk her home when he couldn't. He did his best to take care of everything for Dorothy, to keep her safe, mold her into a better woman, and he kept her isolated until she turned 15. It was then that Raymond left home to go to the military, the hardest decision he ever made.

Dorothy sat on the front porch with her head dug between her legs. She wiped the tear that streaked down her face. Raymond sat next to her and patted her back. She had been crying for three days.

"Do you have to go?" she sniffed as she looked at him.

"I'm sorry, but I have to, Dottie." Raymond sighed and put her head on his shoulders. "You know what, Dorothy?"

"What?"

"I'm gonna go and get stronger, so I can fight all the bad guys for you."

She looked up to him and smiled in delight "Are you sure?!"

"Yes! You're gonna tell them you have a brother who is in the army, and he's very strong. You know how soldiers are. Very strong, and nobody can hurt whoever is close to them. You are my sister, and I am going to protect you."

"So that is why you have to go?"

"Yes, that's why. I have to go and learn how to fight so nobody can bother my lil sis." He pulled her nose, and she laughed.

"Okay, Raymond. But don't forget to send me letters and call me."

"Yes, I will, ma'am… and you make sure not to forget to be a good kid to your mom and take care of your brothers. Also, do well in school and make me proud too."

"I will."

"I believe in you, Dorothy. You are a great young

woman, and you're gonna make me proud."

Dorothy hugged him and started crying again. The one who she could hold on to was leaving her. Things weren't going to be the same with Raymond away.

Dorothy was now a teenager, left alone with Brenda and the boys from hell. Dorothy did not talk to her brothers much; they were mischief's tool. There was nothing to talk about with them. She always thought of them as the kids nobody wanted, like they were simply dropped off at the house one day, and she and her mother were stuck with them.

When she was old enough, Dorothy got a job to take care of her mom. She worked at the local bookstore, which was where she spent most of her time. She did not have many girlfriends, and boys disgusted her.

No one in the family noticed or cared when Dorothy was gone for several days. Brenda did not know her daughter had gotten a job, but that wasn't the only thing she didn't know. Dorothy went through high school as a scholar and exceptional student and finished with the third-highest GPA in her graduating class. Raymond would have been so proud of his little sister. She was doing well academically and in other areas too. She fended for herself and didn't depend on anyone.

Dorothy went on to North Carolina A and T and majored in English with an emphasis on journalism. She excelled in college and began to love the media department. She even hosted a show on the college radio station. For the most part, this blossoming flower stayed to herself. Her roommate in the freshman dorm was a loner, too, so they were a perfect match.

Although her big brother was not there to experience life with her, letters from Raymond kept her going. Dorothy wanted to make the only person in the family who cared for her very proud. She never heard from her mom or other brothers, but that did not stop her. She continued to progress in school; she was a bright student with a bright future ahead of her.

Then all of a sudden, a visitor arrived. During her junior year, Sam showed up at her dorm. Dorothy did not even think he knew she had gone to college. Shocked to see him in her room waiting for her, she looked at him and walked out the door. He followed her and grabbed her hand.

"Baby girl, can we talk?"

"About what? And why now? Why would you show up now when I am doing well without y'all in my life? You never cared for me."

"I deserve that. All of it, but please hear me out. We need to talk now. I should've done this long before now."

"You have 30 minutes, and then I'm leaving."

They went to the local café for coffee and an overdue conversation. Sam started by saying he was sorry for the life he gave her.

"Baby girl, I never meant to be the turmoil in your life. I wasn't ready to be a father or a husband at the time, but your mom was pregnant with your brother, not Raymond. I felt like I had no choice but to marry her though there was no feeling of love whatsoever, and neither was I happy about the pregnancy. At the time, it seemed like marrying her was the right thing to do, but I regretted that decision every day of my life. We co-existed in the house, and the kids kept coming. To avoid coming home, I decided to accept a traveling job where I could be me, living outside of the parameters of being a father or husband. Honestly, she was not who I wanted to be with. When your mom and I met, I was dating another woman at the time, yet your mom was persistent in having me. Even though I was supposed to be committed to someone else, we engaged in sexual relations together, and that kept going on for a few months until I ended it to be with the woman I truly loved. Your mom was heartbroken; she preferred to have a piece of me instead of all of me. The other woman and I moved to the next town and had a great life, but I had an issue with being faithful. She grew tired of me and kicked me out. With nowhere to go, I called Brenda, and she accepted me with open arms. I felt like I was forced to go there, and I hated her for wanting me. She was what men call a loose woman. She didn't care if a man was married or had kids. She destroyed people and families with no regard. Honestly, I never wanted you to hurt, but your mom was a living nightmare which I couldn't stand."

He took a deep breath and continued hesitantly. "You should know that Raymond is not my child. When I moved in with Brenda, Raymond was five years old, and his dad was the local numbers runner. She was only with him for the benefits; once she got pregnant, he left her and Raymond. When I came along, I felt pity for Raymond, so I accepted him as mine. Brenda would party and drink every night while I worked two jobs to keep the household in order. I guess it was my punishment for treating women like used cars. But I married her, and that's when Brenda's behavior reached an all-time low. She would disappear days at a time, leaving me to care for a baby and Raymond. She was the most worthless mother possible and an even worse wife. As time went on, I began to resent her being around. I desired to be with other women, yet I still wanted to be a faithful husband to a faithful wife. I know it sounds kind of crazy, but that was our life. And the kids kept coming. I had doubts about the children, but I still trusted her. I was never abusive to her until you were born. You were born from another man, Raymond's dad. They continued to see each other while I played the good husband, even if only for a short while. I felt pity for her, so I stayed, knowing I did not love her and continued to let her use me. By the time you were born, I was completely done with her. She was gutter trash to me, and I treated her as such. Then reconnected with my ex, whom I yearned for all those years. She lived in Greensboro, so my traveling job was the front for my double life. I made sure Raymond took care of you and you only; I doubted the other kids were mine. I only came back on occasions to make sure you were stable, and I gave Raymond money to make certain you were provided for." He sighed and watched her expression. He truly meant what he said to her. It wasn't good for her to be kept in the dark about who her mother was or the reason why he always physically abused her.

Dorothy sat in amazement, not knowing if she should defend her mother or not. How could she even think such a thought? Brenda didn't care one bit for Dorothy, but it was still hard to hear such horrible things about her. Dorothy's mind was running a mile a minute. She fought to process what was said and connect the dots at the same time. It all made sense now, the reason she acted uncaring towards her, why she endured the beatings calmly and showed such weakness. Dottie remembered her words when she was a kid. She was getting punished for what she had done because she deserved it.

"Dottie, I want to apologize for attacking your mother. The day you saw me throw her across the room, she'd pulled the last straw. She called me to come home. Although she knew of the woman I was staying with; she frequently called me there; I guess we had an unspoken understanding. That day her voice was shattering. She was stuttering in her speech. She belted out, "Come quick, Sam! Dorothy's over here sluttin' around at school!" I didn't want to believe what she said because you were so young. However, I thought her habits might have trickled down to you. You see, I have always had a soft spot for you, and she knew I would come for you or Raymond, so she took that to her advantage. When I arrived, she told me the real reason she called me over was because she was let go from her job for screwing in the house where she cared for an elderly patient. She slept with the patient's son, who was half her age. I gathered that they told her to leave immediately. She was scared to tell me because she knew I would be furious, and I was indeed. You could almost see the flames from the pit of my heart. I wanted her to suffer for the harm she caused so many people. She lied to me, so I would come home, and even worse, she was whoring around again. Dottie, I want you to know I never wanted to hurt you. I am deeply sorry for the pain you endured. You deserve to know the truth."

Hearing the nickname Dottie took her back to her childhood. She was drenched in tears and at a loss for words. Finally, she opened her eyes and looked at him and asked the only words she could muster.

"Where is my biological father? Who is he? I don't understand why this was kept a secret, and why the sudden urge to tell me now?" It felt strange to her. Why didn't anybody bother to tell her before? She could have accepted the fact and moved on better, instead of now when she was doing better with life on her own.

"Dottie, I wanted to tell you when you were younger, but your mom feared you would get off track. You are the brightest out of all the kids. I wish you were my own. I wasn't much of a father, but I hope that you can forgive me. Your mom pleaded for me not to come to see you, but I had to release the truth in order for me to move forward. I am divorcing your mom and moving away. Dottie, I know you will be fine. You are a strong woman. This will only make you stronger. I am certain Brenda will be calling you; please hear her out. The truth needs to be heard from her as well as an apology. After all these years, I am not bitter or angry anymore, and your brothers are not in jail yet, thankfully. Raymond, as you already know, is doing well, blossoming in the military. He's in Korea now. I am sure you still get his letters and packages. I am leaving you with this. It should get you through your last year of school. I love you, Dottie." He patted her on the shoulder and got up to leave.

She sat in silence, holding the envelope and searching for words. Her mother never told her who she was or who her father was. The man who had ruined her life had also redeemed it. Dorothy didn't know what sentiment she should be experiencing. So many were vying for attention. She managed to hold his hand as one lone tear made its way down his face.

As they parted company, Dorothy was in a state of shock and disbelief, wondering where to go from here. She spoke to Brenda earlier that day, and she did not say anything about this unexpected visit.

Dorothy needed to get Raymond on the phone, but the only number she had was no longer in service. She cried out "WHY??????????"

All her life, she consumed the pain and the hurt and brokenness. She was having a breakdown no one was ready for. Dorothy isolated herself, refusing to take calls from anyone, especially Brenda.

After a week, Dorothy finally opened the envelope Sam gave her. In it was $5000 and a picture of her and Raymond as a child. She looked at the picture and asked, "What did I do to deserve shitty parents, a coward of a mother and dad who could not take a look at me?"

Dorothy finally called her mom. Brenda could not get a word in edgewise over the stern yelling coming from Dorothy.

"You filthy Jezebel. I hated Daddy because of your stupid, adulterous ways! What do you have to say for yourself, and while you are thinking, who is my real father? Do you have any idea how much this hurts? You dirty piece of crap! You are not a mother; you are a Jezebel! How many men were there? Do you even know? Go ahead! No need to be quiet now. Talk! Act like you care for once in your life."

Just as Brenda began to speak, there was a distinct silence that let her know that Dorothy had hung up the phone.

Dorothy dropped out of college that year. She went on a downward path, becoming the woman her mom was, using men as a tool. Whatever she needed, she got it from men, no matter what it took. Raymond lost control of Dorothy, and he was not close enough to reel her in. He thought she could be the one to break that generational curse, but he was wrong.

"Dorothy…"

"What do you want?" she cut in sharply.

"Listen to me, Dorothy…."

"I am not the same ten-year-old girl anymore, Raymond," she cut in again.

"You need to listen to me. What's going on with you, Dorothy?"

"It is none of your business. It's my life, so don't act like you care about me now."

"I know you're mad at me for hiding things from you, but they weren't worth saying. It wouldn't have helped you to hear that we were a dysfunctional family who pretended to be okay on the outside. Or that mom was cheating around with men or that dad had another family on the other side of town."

"But you should have told me. You were my best friend, Ray! We told each other everything, and you promised you would never hide anything from me!"

"I'm sorry, Dorothy… I…"

"I don't want to have anything to do with you anymore. You are all the same, wicked and heartless people. I don't need you anymore, so don't ever call me again!" she slammed the phone on the table and buried her face in the pillows screaming on top of her lungs.

Dorothy stopped taking Raymond's calls because he knew the secrets and never told her. She blamed everyone else for the problems in her life. The once studious college student was now a bomb that was about to explode from the many years of suffering. So she masked her pain with whatever or whoever would help bury who she really was.

She depended on the many men she met until Clint came along. They were just cordial for a few weeks before moving forward. She was not ready for any commitment or a man to tell her what to do, but she figured Clint could help her take care of her daughter, Charlie. Dorothy honestly didn't know who Charlie's father was. She was becoming her mother all over again.

After Clint had been living with Dorothy for a few months, travesty hit, and Brenda passed away. Dorothy had not spoken to her mom much over the years. She hated her for the things she did and did not say to her.

At first she was not going to attend the funeral, but she changed her mind at the last minute. She didn't want to have any regrets, despite how she was treated.

Dorothy arrived at the funeral in her old beat-up car with a baby in tow. She saw her dad, her brothers, and Raymond. Acknowledging them with a head nod, she sat on the other side of the chapel and didn't say a word.

Raymond tried to talk to his sister, but she was full of rage.

"Dorothy,"

She eyed him then turned to look away.

"How are you doing?"

"Better as I could ever be," she said curtly.

"Do you mind?" he asked, pointing to the empty chair next to her.

"Suit yourself."

He sat next to her and sighed. It had been a long time since they talked. She was much different now. More mature, beautiful and accompanied by a cute little girl who had Brenda's eyes. How did she get the child; he was surprised.

"How have you been?"

"Obviously good."

"Dorothy, I am sorry about all that has happened. I know you were hurt that I kept you in the dark about Sam not being your real father. I honestly don't know who your real father is. I am so sorry about that. He paused and looked at his sister, who was trying hard to fight back the tears that were streaming down her face.

"When I knew that Sam wasn't our dad and that we had the same father, I was angry at mom, but I didn't want you to go through the hurt of knowing what was going on in the house. That was why I decided to take care of you myself. The sudden treats and trips were my idea of not letting you see the mess both Brenda and Sam were in."

Dorothy wiped the tears from her face but didn't look at her brother. Maneuvering her head not to meet his eyes, Dorothy gave Raymond a side hug. She wished it wasn't real; she wished they were a happy family, with a real father and mother and wonderful siblings. She pulled away gently and beckoned for Charlie to follow her.

Dorothy vanished and never looked back on her family. She was with her baby, Charlie, broke and living life hopelessly. She knew she needed a provider for Charlie so she could live her life as she wanted, so she wooed Clint, and he moved in with them. And the cycle continued.

Charlie's New Beginnings

Now that you understand how Dorothy came to be so broken, let me get back to Charlie. Let me tell you about Charlie as a young girl starting elementary school. You see, she did not look like other little girls. Charlie was a girl with a round, pale face and a sympathetic expression from her small, brown eyes. Her small head had very untamed, chestnut brown hair. Skinny as a nail you could pierce through the wall. Her brown skin glowed from the Vaseline that was plastered all over her face. Her hair was braided in two pigtails, and her clothes were outdated, shabby, and slightly moth-eaten in places. Her shoes weren't fit to walk in. You could see her toes peeping from the top of her shoes. She looked unkempt from head to toe.

From the outside, you would see a hot mess; on the inside, she carried the weight of a world on her heart. She did not speak. It kind of seemed like she was lost in her own thoughts most of the time.

Dorothy did not think school was important for Charlie; it was a waste of time for Dorothy to take her every day. Although she attended school since five, Charlie did not become aware of a schedule until Clint came along. She was not in her proper grade level either. Charlie was an eight-year-old struggling in the second grade with little hope of making it to third grade.

School was definitely an escape from the hectic life at home; she could be around other kids, different kids. Unfortunately, she did not make many friends, and the friends she did have were just as awkward as she was. They were misfits trying to fit into a sea of cool kids, kids with clothing that was pressed and primped, and hair that was fried from the hot comb so fresh you could still smell the sulfur. The more she tried to make friends, the more they stayed away from her. That is until Nikki, the new girl, came on the scene.

The class was at recess, and Nikki was hanging with the new kids. She had strong confidence in herself. Nikki was vibrant and popular, but she was a year younger than Charlie. Nothing similar in their characteristics, but Charlie thought if she were to be accepted by Nikki, others would accept her too.

Nikki's skin was flawless, the color of a caramel apple, and her hair was long and flowing. She was bold in her speech and was feared by her classmates. Charlie wanted to embody the person Nikki was; she was in awe of her. A bit nervous about getting Nikki's attention, Charlie hoped the friendship with Nikki would be the boost she needed. Yet, she had no idea that Nikki was carrying the same baggage as everyone else in her life, a disturbed little girl who covered the hate inside with boldness.

Charlie took her shot and approached Nikki. She raised her head and looked Nikki straight in her eyes.

"Hi, my name is Charlie. Would you like to swing with me?" Nikki gave her a growl before responding and then suddenly softened. "Why, not. My name is Nikki Shaw. What's yours?"

"Charlotte, but everyone calls me Charlie."

"Are you in my class?"

"Yes."

"How come I don't see you?" Nikki sat on the swing next to her. She knew everybody in the class, but she had never seen Charlie.

"I'm always in class, but I don't talk much, though."

"Well, we're friends now." Nikki smiled at her. For the first time, Charlie got a friend she could talk to. All the other kids didn't want to be friends with her.

She remembered the day she tried to talk to her classmates. It was recess, and she was sitting alone at the playground

"Hi," Charlie said, smiling shyly, stretching her hand for a handshake.

"What do you want?" The brown-haired girl looked up at her and stood up.

"I… I… am Charlie. I…I… would like to j…j…join you."

"No, you can't."

"Why? I just want to play."

"This place isn't for people like you," she said and pushed Charlie back.

Charlie sadly went back to sit alone and watched them play. None of the kids wanted to play with her or even talk to her. The opportunity she got to talk to Nikki was one she never imagined. Charlie saw her as the first person who willingly became friends with her.

From that time on, Nikki and Charlie were best friends. Everyone called them the modern-day Dennis the Menis times 2. She and Nikki caused many problems with other kids in school. Nikki was the antidote Charlie did not need, but Nikki gave her something no one else did, love and attention that was not forced. Nikki was what Charlie needed to break out of her shyness.

The two girls would meet up at school, not to do schoolwork but to raise hell amongst their peers. They repeatedly attacked kids for their food, making them give away their lunch. Soon they were fighting every day. Charlie was once suspended for slapping a boy who called her dirty. Nikki was not too far behind her. She was sent home for a few days for beating a girl with a shoe.

Although they were friends who went about making mischief, their bad behavior made them quite popular in school. Nikki was the motivator, and Charlie followed Nikki's instructions.

Nikki was born in Raleigh, North Carolina, Nikkita Allen, to a drug-addict mother named Jackie. Nikki did not know her mom as a small baby; Jackie was not able to keep any of her kids. She lived in a motel where she used drugs and practiced prostitution as a way of life. Jackie didn't even know her own self. She definitely couldn't raise a child, so Nikki became a ward of the state.

The young girl bounced around from birth to age six. Finally, after six years of being in the system, a nice family from Durham, North Carolina, adopted her.

The Shaw family had two kids of their own in addition to the three foster kids. Nikki was the last child added to the Shaw family and the youngest of the clan. The Shaws, the family everyone adored, was nothing like the perfect family they portrayed themselves to be. They made their money and business from adopting kids. They wore the coolest flyaway collars and the hippest platform shoes. The cars were exceptional: the candy apple red El Camino, the Midnight Black Ford Mustang as the family car, and the emerald green Chevy Chevelle. Yes, they were pimping battered kids for monetary gain.

Nikki was reared to fall in line with the other kids, the little toy soldiers. Betty Jean, Nikki's foster mom, was a small-built yet demanding woman; her husband Larry was a towering fellow but unusually timid, a match of no other kind. Betty Jean ruled the house while Larry sat and watched and worked.

Betty ran her house like a small prison camp. They rose early in the morning for morning chores, from scrubbing the walls to hand-washing laundry, then off to school they would go. Many days food for them was an oversight. They were often hungry and bruised from the beatings they would get for being disobedient.

Despite trying, Nikki could not follow directions. She wanted to do what *she* wanted to do, so she was locked away many days for not following orders. Her punishment was to provide sexual favors for the older brother while the others watched. School was her escape from the Shaw household, which she called the dungeon.

It was at school where she would cause havoc on other kids in order to mask her own pain. She picked on kids who were weaker than she was and those who she felt could be intimidated. With Charlie as her accomplice, which made her mission much easier.

A Blossoming Friendship

C harlie and Nikki are now both in the fourth grade, two peas in a pod and destructive, to say the least. If you saw Charlie, you saw Nikki and vice versa. Nothing tore them apart. Neither was mature enough to discuss their troubled childhood, even though they had similar problems. They were two tattered vessels that needed a rapture to save them, not knowing that the baggage they were carrying brought them together. They decided to ignore the ugly demons they both were fighting with. At least they were happy outside of the homes where they lived.

They only saw each other at school; neither was allowed outside guests at their homes. The girls could not wait for Mondays to come, so they could be reunited. Nikki spent her weekends locked away from her siblings. She reeked from not bathing because she was so unruly. She may have received a meal once throughout the weekend. Before the start of school on Monday morning, she was allowed to bathe and eat a full meal. If she showed up to school looking unkempt, the Shaw's gravy train would end.

Charlie, on the other hand, was going through a similar shame and disgrace over the weekend. Although she was fed, she was not fed with love. Her siblings continued to abuse her.

School days were a sign of relief for them. Each day would be a different fight with anyone who interfered in the girls' daily mischief. No other kids wanted to be around them.

Nikki would purposely pick on kids if they seemed to be better than her. She was a bully you didn't dare to challenge. Charlie would follow along; soon, she was no longer the shy little freak the kids knew.

Charlie would start fights so Nikki could slander a child and then beat him to a bloody pulp. Charlie would tell the kids not to tell anyone; otherwise, they would get a worse beating.

Neither of the girls did much schoolwork. They were always in trouble, but it did not matter because they would still be in trouble at home. Teachers feared them because they were so horrible and because the parents never returned their calls. Not a single teacher met their parents. The work the girls turned in was poorly done, and they had no future beyond elementary school.

As they grew older, their bond grew as well. They managed to get out of elementary and middle school on a wing and a prayer and were on to high school. This was where Charlie met Mrs. Dempsey, the high school principal. She slowly got to know pieces of Charlie's story, yet she could not pry Charlie away from Nikki. Mrs. Dempsey was a voice Charlie needed, a voice that would later be the best part of her life. She tried to reel Charlie in when Charlie was at school, but the young terror skipped school so much Mrs. Dempsey had a difficult time with her.

High school was different for the two girls; they were not the top dogs anymore. Many other kids were just as disturbed as them, and they would soon meet their match. The bullying would not be as great in high school, or it would be war. To avoid the hopelessness dominating high school, they started to skip school or sleep through class.

Both Charlie and Nikki had blossomed into very attractive girls on the outside. Still, boys could not see past their rough demeanor. Their dark skin was proven to shine amongst their peers. They may have been gorgeous on the outside, but inside they were the ugliest girls around.

They turned their anger into being the class clowns, even though they did not have classes together. Charlie did not care for school much since she entered high school. Mrs. Dempsey worked diligently to show Charlie another way, but it was hard to combat Nikki's influence.

It was a chilly October day, and the new semester of junior year had just begun. The girls started the day taking public transportation to the lower side of Charlotte. It was their hang-out spot when they did not go to school. That was where they met with Dwight Thomas, an older guy who enjoyed the lust of younger girls. Dwight was tall, stunning, and light-skinned like a white chocolate bar. He had a goatee and smelled like the rustic woods of a forest.

Dwight hid his age from the girls. He had a close eye on Charlie; he noticed she was a bit more reserved than Nikki. Although some of Charlie's shyness was broken, she still had a meek and mild demeanor about her and could be easily persuaded. That was why she and Nikki made it so long as friends. Nikki could control Charlie. Charlie was desperate for friendship, so Nikki took advantage of that, and Charlie did not know she was under Nikki's spell.

Dwight knew Nikki adored him, but he also knew Nikki would be trouble, so he set his eyes on Charlie. He was going to get Charlie whether she wanted him or not.

Charlie and Nikki carried on their day with Dwight and a few friends. Charlie drifted off by herself to be alone for a moment. She was sitting on the steps of the apartment complex they visited. Nikki was so engulfed with her laughter and the gossip of the girls who had baby daddies. Nikki loved that excitement and the drama that came with it. Charlie was never impressed with that kind of drama. While Charlie was sitting by herself, Dwight came along and sat beside her. Charlie was timid at first, but she couldn't resist the snake charmer.

Dwight was on baby number two at nineteen years old. He gave Charlie the attention she desired. She grew comfortable talking to him, and he began to caress her back. Charlie felt uneasy and knew something was not right. She stood to find Nikki. Nikki protected her. He grabbed Charlie by her legs, took her hands, and pushed her stomach, lowering her down to his lap. Charlie began to cry out, but he covered her mouth. The tears started flowing from her eyes as memories of sexual abuse flooded her mind.

That creep took his other hand and placed it on her sweet nectar. Then his fingers entered the fresh fruit of desire. Charlie, trying to get away, tears flowing, wanted to scream but couldn't. He uttered to her, "You know you want this, the lean meat of new possibilities." Dwight then picked Charlie up, took her to the stoop, and began to take her clothes off, smoothing his hands over her young breast, injecting his lean meat inside her.

Charlie had nowhere to go and no one to save her as he stroked his body against hers. He got up and left her there, bruised, broken, and bewildered. Dwight raped Charlie without remorse or guilt. She sat there, drowning in her tears. Clothing ripped, her hair full of muss and dirt, and her body was covered with an odor of fear. As she tried to collect her shirt and jeans, she became weaker and weaker. She could not gather herself. All she could do was think maybe she deserved to be treated this way, the same way Roxy took her innocence.

Nikki found Charlie unclothed, bloody, and weeping. She was shocked to see Charlie that way, shaking as she tried to gain her balance on the wall. Charlie mouthed some words to her, but her head could not process anything she was saying. Nikki was in utter disbelief, but she left Charlie there, helpless. The best friend Charlie needed at that time just walked away.

Charlie finally pulled herself together and walked home to wash away the embarrassment. Her legs felt heavy, and her heart sank. Nikki left her alone and didn't even look back to help her. Charlie cried hard as she scrubbed her body down until she bled. Why would my best friend leave me like that? Did she tell Dwight to do this to me?

The once strong friendship was no more. Charlie did not hear from Nikki for days. She was not at school; Nikki just disappeared. Charlie was unsure of why the only friend she had left her in a desperate state. She wanted answers; why did Nikki run? Did she know about what Dwight did to her? Charlie went to Nikki's house, called her, and waited for Nikki to show up. Days, weeks, and months went by. No sign of Nikki anywhere. Charlie was left feeling betrayed by the only friend that considered her as an equal. Nikki never called nor appeared in school.

Unbeknownst to Charlie, Nikki was struggling as much as her former friend. She took the blame for Charlie being raped. In her mind, she was so interested in Dwight that she forced Charlie to go with her to meet him, but she didn't know that Dwight was going to do a very terrible thing to her best friend.

The one person she fought to protect was hurt by her actions. Nikki soon became the image of her biological mother, Jackie. A lost girl trying to be a woman at 16 years old, dropping out of school, selling her body, stripping and doing heavy drugs to cover up her guilt.

The once best friends never talked about their common struggles, the similarities of mothers, and the sexual and verbal abuse. For some reason, Nikki thought Charlie was different from her. They avoided the hurtful parts of their lives, but they had more in common than they knew.

Charlie carried on as if nothing happened. Mrs. Dempsey knew how troubled Charlie was, so Mrs. Dempsey guided Charlie through the last year of school. However, she had no idea what she was to do next, just as Nikki did not have any future. They both were walking through life aimlessly, looking for someone to love them.

First Love

Trying to forget her past life with no one to talk to, Charlie saw a television commercial for a trade school, a possibility she never considered. Her mentor, Mrs. Walker, encouraged Charlie to do something and stop feeling sorry for herself.

"You can do this, Charlie; I know you can."

"No, I can't. I can't do this, Mrs. Walker."

"Charlie, no one is always at their best. Sometimes, it is smooth sailing. We feel energized, make progress, and feel grateful and confident." She sat opposite Charlie.

"I'll just do this and…"

"You are not just gonna do this Charlie, you are going to do this and enjoy it. No matter what you are facing, it's not the end of the world, and you can make it."

Charlie looked at her. She was going to try doing something new in her life. Mrs. Walker reminded Charlie that despite the odds, she could achieve her goals.

Charlie enrolled in an 18-month program in medical administration. This may have been the only thing Charlie tried to accomplish in life; she owed it to herself to make something positive happen. All seemed to be going well, and classes were moving along. Charlie learned to manage independently, interacting only with the people she spoke to at school.

This new young woman received no motivation from her mom, who was seldom present. Even though Charlie was older, she still fought those demons that were embedded in her thoughts. Her routine was school and home; her transportation was the city bus. On her daily route, she met Donna, another student in the medical field.

Donna was well experienced in life and had her own apartment. One day after class, Donna invited Charlie over for drinks. This was the first time Charlie had a drink of alcohol. They quickly became good friends, and Charlie began to spend most of the time studying at Donna's apartment. Soon, she moved in with Donna and obtained her first job, truly getting control of her life.

One weekend, Donna had a dinner party with friends from school and people she'd met around town. Donna introduced Charlie to Malik, a technology major at DeVry University. He was a highly educated young man who held an impressive conversation.

He was short in stature, yet his confidence made him appear taller. He was attentive and dressed like a contemporary of Bobby Seale or another member of the Black Panther Party for Self-defense. He was just tall enough to reach Charlie's shoulder in his all-black and fight the power mantra.

"Hi, I am Malik. It is a pleasure to make your acquaintance. I must say your eyes are captivating, and your smile is breathtaking. Would you mind engaging in conversation with me?"

Talking under her breath, Charlie wondered who he was. A dude with all this confidence wanted to talk to her? But she only smiled and tried to be friendly. She responded, "It is nice to meet you as well, and thank you for the compliment. I would be delighted to converse with you."

"Thank you for such an honor. It's a great privilege."

Malik was very friendly. Even when Charlie was feeling hesitant to talk to him, he immediately noticed and made her feel better.

Charlie was unsure as to why someone like him would want to meet her. They had nothing in common. From the first meeting, Charlie's mind began to wander. Her past compelled her not to trust people. Yet, he made her smile and feel safe. It took a while for Charlie to agree to go out with him. All she could think of was Dwight pressing his skin against hers. But Malik was more interested in getting to know Charlie.

They talked and laughed into the late hours nearly every night since their first meeting. Charlie was impressed with his calm tone and his thoughts; he did not want anything from Charlie but her conversation. Their friendship soon grew into a relationship, Charlie's first love.

After a while, they were inseparable; he would escort her to school and work, making sure she was safe. There was nothing sexual between them, though. Charlie was falling in love with Malik. He was someone she never had in her life. He gave her the love and attention she deserved. Making her feel more safe than she had ever been in her life. Of course, she found it hard to believe him at first. Was he in her life to break her again? Or was he there to use her and leave?

Against her negative judgement, she began to trust Malik, trusting him and falling head over heels. They soon gave each the connection of love, their bodies intertwined as one. He was gentle, he understood her needs and how she needed to be touched. Malik remained after their connection; he held her giving her the satisfaction she desired. He made her feel like a woman, a woman to be loved and cherished. What more could Charlie ask for? This was the first time she ever felt what it was to be loved and given attention.

Malik cared for Charlie as if she was his only priority in life. Charlie flourished in trade school, completing the first few classes of the program in record timing. Malik helped Charlie study and guided her through classes. He was nearly finished with his degree and wanted to secure his future. Although they were only together for a short time, Malik wanted to marry Charlie. He knew his life would not be the same without her. She was the woman he wanted, gentle, reserved, and understanding. He couldn't afford to lose her for anything in the world. He could imagine the future with her each day he was with her.

In hopes of proposing, Malik set everything in place. The whole gang was there, and he asked Charlie to be his bride.

"Will you walk with me on a journey of no regrets where we will both grow old with grey hair and be happy till the end of time?"

"What do you mean, Malik?"

"What I'm saying, Charlie, is will you marry me?"

Charlie was dumbstruck. She never expected to be proposed to. She looked around at the people cheering her on to say yes, but regrettably, Charlie declined.

Malik was crushed, his heart shredded in a million pieces. Charlie was fearful of marriage, fearful of making a commitment to Malik. He never knew of Charlie's upbringing; he did not know of the rape because she kept that part of her life deeply buried in the recesses of her mind. Charlie did not want to hurt Malik, who humbly accepted the rejection and continued the friendship with Charlie, hoping she would change her mind.

After a while, Malik found interest in another young lady. He continued to see Charlie and the other young lady too.

Malik, who usually walked Charlie home after class, didn't meet her this particular afternoon, so Charlie proceeded on her way home. To her surprise, Malik was waiting for the bus with another woman. When he saw Charlie, he did not move. He did not even acknowledge Charlie. He pretended as if Charlie was a figment of his imagination.

Wallowing in self-pity, Charlie walked on to her lonely apartment with thoughts of being rejected yet again by someone she loved and trusted. Charlie was rejected by so many people in her life: the family that should've loved her, a mother who abandoned her emotionally, a best friend who walked away from her when she was weak and vulnerable, and now the first man she was willingly intimate with left her broken and confused.

Charlie did not understand her life. Why wasn't she ever good enough for people who claimed to love her? Charlie fell deep into the bottom of her life. Malik never reached out to Charlie. After she made numerous calls to him, he vanished as if she never existed.

Charlie dropped out of school, quit her job, and moved back in with her verbally abusive mom, a place where she didn't need to be. Out of work and nowhere to go, she fell into a deep depression with no direction in life.

After months of feeling sorry for herself, Charlie obtained a job at a local restaurant, but she barely went to work. She gained a great deal of weight. Food was the medicine that calmed her spirit.

Oddly enough, Charlie began to feel ill in the mornings. Curious to know why she felt so bad, Charlie went to the clinic. She was pregnant with Malik's baby. In desperation, Charlie aborted the baby without any help or support, a decision she regretted the rest of her life.

Destruction

Charlie wasn't well; she was on her fifth job within a year, her mom was still verbally destroying her mind, calling her everything from trash to a failure in life. So, Charlie packed her bags, took the blue vase her mom tried to shatter, and never looked back.

She ended up in a few shelters for a while. Then, a co-worker needed a roommate, and Charlie jumped at the opportunity, determined to get her life on track.

Things began to get better for Charlie. She purchased her first car, the first major accomplishment in her life. She was trying to heal, and then she met Reggie, a tall, handsome young man who was a little bit older than Charlie. From their first meeting, he adored Charlie. He was not the type of man Charlie fancied, but he possessed a sense of a warrior. Reggie was the gold chain-wearing, gold teeth sporting hoodrat. Charlie may have grown up in the projects, but she tried to stay clear of men like that.

Reggie was so different from Malik. This time Charlie went full throttle with Reggie. She thought if she moved at a faster pace with Reggie, he would not leave her.

When you saw Reggie, you saw Charlie; they did not do much of anything without one another. Charlie maintained her job; Reggie, on the other hand, was an up-and-coming street pharmacist. Charlie never asked what his occupation was. She was just delighted to know someone gave her some attention. Reggie needed Charlie; he required the innocent and sweet look for his business. Charlie did not see the evil she was about to embark upon.

Reggie would drive Charlie to work (in Charlie's car) and pick her up when work was over. Charlie did not go to her apartment much. She either stayed with Reggie at his parent's house, or they rented motels.

There wasn't much to their relationship. He used her car for transportation, and she was too damaged to tell him no. So he stayed on the run, running here and there using her car so much that she could not go anywhere. Charlie would do anything to please Reggie, yet he treated her horribly and controlled her every move. He wanted to know exactly where she was at all times.

She would often do a pick-up or a drop-off alone, never asking what was being delivered. He could tell her to kill someone, and she probably would have done it. Reggie knew how to persuade her to undertake the grimiest assignments, giving her the fake assurance of love.

Charlie did not have a social life nor many friends. Her roommate was not a friend, just someone who needed help paying part of the rent. She did not talk to her family outside of her mother, so Charlie depended on Reggie to give her direction. He knew she was weak and lacked self-esteem, an easy mark for him to control. They were the modern-day Black Bonnie and Clyde.

Instead of getting into Reggie's product, Charlie sought alcohol as her drug of choice. Charlie would go to work reeking of whatever she could find to drink, slowly becoming a functioning alcoholic.

Reggie was too occupied to notice. He was seeing other women, even bringing the other women around Charlie. He would pick Charlie up from work with the other women in her car. They would drop Charlie off, and Reggie would not return until a few days later. Charlie would walk to work or get there the best way she could. Reggie took advantage of her sickness. He never intended to truly love Charlie, just saw her as a tool he could use to get whatever he wanted anytime he needed it.

The final straw was when Reggie took Charlie's rent money and the roommates' rent money and spent it. When they realized the money was gone, Reggie was nowhere to be found. Without being seen, he dropped Charlie's car off at her workplace. Charlie's roommate kicked her out; even though Charlie was barely there, she was still paying rent. Charlie trusted Reggie with the rent money being gullible and naïve, not thinking Reggie would betray her. Charlie found herself in a drunken stupor, on the side of the road crying. She had no clue where she was. Reggie was gone, and Charlie was left all used up and homeless.

She could not go back to work to face her roommate. Charlie did not want to go back to her raging mom, so she lived in her car for a month. She sold her body and any other material items she had. She needed a refuge, so she started the car and headed south. North Carolina was a past she wanted to forget. A place that had been the beginning of her pains, she was ready to leave there and start a new life.

Brand New

Although all the abuse, ruined childhood, and the failed relationships were over, Charlie wanted to withdraw from that part of life. She had had enough of the hurt she bottled in for years. She needed a new lease on life, anything that could make her disregard her toxic life. Charlie recalled her old high school principal, who helped her graduate. She reached out to Mrs. Dempsey and found out that she moved to Florida the year Charlie graduated high school and was offered a position to run an all-girl reform school.

Mrs. Dempsey had a sweet spot for Charlie and was delighted to have Charlie come to Florida.

"Charlie darling! How're you doing?" Mrs. Dempsey said eagerly over the phone.

"I'm… okay" she couldn't say the word good. It had never been part of her dictionary nor her experiences in life. She sniffed as she talked to Mrs. Dempsey.

"No worries, Charlie; it's going to be okay. I promise." She was going to help Charlie. She had always wanted to, and now she had the opportunity to help her mold her broken vessel. To make her shine and find happiness in life. She sent Charlie money for travel and food, and Charlie was on her way. Florida was soon to be her new home. She did not tell anyone she left; besides, no one cared, not even her mother would if she had known.

She set out for a ten-hour drive and thankfully reached her destination. Mrs. Dempsey and her husband welcomed Charlie with open arms. They never had children, but they invested their lives into helping young people.

They opened their home to Charlie, gave her some time to get situated and devise a plan for her life.

"Welcome to our home Charlie." Mrs. Dempsey hugged her tight.

For the first time, Charlie felt what it was like to feel welcomed and loved. Mrs. Dempsey wasn't her mother, but she felt like one.

A month went by, and the Dempsey's coached and mentored Charlie. First, she had to rid her system of alcohol. They thought a month would be enough time for Charlie to gather her thoughts and refresh her mind. They hired Charlie at the reform school as a mail clerk. They required her to pay them $100.00 a month, maintain her car, and budget to save money. Charlie was forced to receive counseling for her problems, so the pain didn't manifest itself into something more damaging. Even though she was in another state, the pain was still there.

"Hello, Charlie," the therapist said as she sat opposite her

"Hello."

"How do you feel?"

"I don't know."

"You can talk to me," the therapist said calmly.

"Why should I?"

"Because I can help you."

Charlie eyed her and closed her eyes. She couldn't be helped. The hate she had received in her life was far more than anyone could imagine.

"You gotta help yourself first, Charlie, in order for me to help you. It's got to start with you first," the therapist still remained calm and unmoved.

"Will you just let me be? There is no way you can help me. You don't know what I've been through. You have no idea of any of it at all!"

"That is why I want to help you, to get you out of that hurt," she smiled at Charlie. She needed to gain her trust. "You see, Charlie, I may not know what you have been through in your life, but I want you to know that you can get out of the pain you have been through all these years. Each of us has our own dark scars we carry, but they will only weigh us down if we dwell on them. I know it's hard; I understand that it's difficult, but trust me, I can help you. But first, the change has to begin with you."

Through counseling and therapy, Charlie progressed slowly. She found it hard to open up to the therapist at first. Memories of the hurt, pain, neglect and abuse came up. It was hard remembering those incidents, so she spent most of her time working. She had no social life or friends; she buried herself in her work. Sadly, she was still deeply depressed, she could not trust anyone and definitely wasn't going to try love again.

The therapist encouraged Charlie to join a group for battered women, and Mrs. Dempsey continued to guide Charlie. Most importantly, she was a parent to Charlie. Even though Charlie was an adult, she needed guidance and structure.

"Why do you help me, Mrs. Dempsey?" Charlie questioned her.

"Because I see a woman of great potential in front of me. I see her flourishing and blooming to become who God wants her to be."

"I am nothing like what you described. Take a look at me! There is nothing left in me!"

"You know something, Charlie?"

"What?"

"A broken heart feels like a billion daggers piercing you at every moment, at every turn with nothing to stop it. Your eyes are dull, smiles fade, and it seems like nothing good is coming to you. Your heart is full of sorrow, remembering the pain each day, and you can't help but cry all night and day. Although you pretend to be okay, deep down, you are shattered. You want someone to be there to hold you, cry with you, and tell you everything will be alright. But you must always remember to get back up no matter what happens. Be strong through all that happens to you. You have to rise up and get rid of that fear that lingers in your mind that you can't become a better person. The change begins with you."

Charlie looked at Mrs. Dempsey and felt hope, something she hadn't felt in a long time.

"Charlie, there is a great light in you, and it never left. You are like gold," Mrs. Dempsey walked slowly to sit on a chair. "You know, before you can get to see the beauty of gold, it has to pass through processes, processes that will make it shiny and glowing for everyone to see. Charlie, all that you have passed through were processes. Processes to make you become shining, strong and dazzling in glory. I know you have been through a lot, but you have to remember that you haven't fulfilled that reason God brought you into this world. If everything was smooth sailing, you probably would have been a wreck and died or even not have this opportunity. So, Charlie, I am not helping you because I want something in return but because I am never giving up on you. Never!' She smiled and sipped the tea in her mug.

Charlie was the daughter Mrs. Dempsey never had, and she was ready to make sure that Charlie became a better person. Charlie continued to attend the therapy sessions and her support group until she was ready to open up.

Charlie met Miranda at one of the support group sessions. Miranda was an older yet a very immature woman. Miranda had four kids; she was very loud and not ashamed to speak her truth.

"Nobody can look down on me unless I want them to," she said to Charlie one day after their session.

"What do you mean?"

Miranda looked at Charlie and burst out laughing. "C'mon… I don't mean I'm going to beat them up or anything."

"I didn't say you were."

"The look on your face did. What I meant was, I don't let anyone belittle me. If they do, it's because I allow them to."

"I don't get it. You can't avoid people from coming into your life and thinking a certain way about you."

"Yes, I can't, but I won't allow them to treat me like trash. The reason people treat you badly is that you allow them to. You have portrayed yourself as someone they can belittle, so that is why they do. I don't mean you have to be rude, but stick to it if you stand for something. Be sure of your decisions and know what you want. I hear from most people that I am loud and stuff, but that's their opinion of what they feel about me. That's not how I see about myself, so I don't let them dictate my life for me. I do my own things myself. Although I need help, I don't show myself as vulnerable" she looked at Charlie. "Do you get it now?"

"Yeah," Charlie muttered slowly, "But you can't resist those people trying to break you?"

Miranda sighed "Sometimes, the people who broke you can be the ones to heal you back. One way or the other, they'll lead you to your healing. You can heal; you just have to believe in yourself first before you can believe in others."

Even though she didn't agree with all of Miranda's philosophies on life, Charlie learned from Miranda to take control of her actions and accept that some of the people she allowed in her life resulted from her own decisions. It was time to submit to the healing process and move forward to growth.

Charlie began to open up about her past with her therapist; they started to experience some real breakthroughs.

"I felt very lonely. Everybody hated me," she said to her therapist in one of the sessions. Most of the sessions were about Charlie talking about sexual abuse and rape. Charlie rarely spoke about the rape to anyone. She felt embarrassed about being raped. That incident left her feeling worthless and unwanted.

"It's okay, Charlie, hiding from those fears will only make you continue to live in them."

Malik was the only person Charlie actually wanted to be close to, yet he abandoned her. Charlie blamed Malik for most of her hurt, not accepting that she was hurting long before Malik entered her life. His absence only intensified the hurt.

The sessions were going well, and Charlie was beginning to feel better about herself. She was looking forward to her meetings, and the healing was opening up new adventures for her.

"How do you feel now, Charlie?"

"I feel good, better."

That was the first time she used the words 'good' and 'better' freely. She smiled more often now. She was getting at peace with herself little by little.

Charlie saved enough money to get her own apartment, yet was she ready to be alone?

"Mrs. Dempsey, thank you for all the support and the love. I really appreciate everything you all have done for me," she paused and looked at Mrs. Dempsey and her husband. "I feel it's time I stay on my own now."

"What do you mean, Charlie?"

"I mean I want to get an apartment of my own now...."

"Charlie darling, have we done anything to hurt you?

"No, no, you haven't, I just feel that I am better now, and I can handle things on my own. So, I am ready to move on."

"Wait a minute, Charlie, are you really ready to move on?"

"Yes, Mrs. Dempsey"

"You know one thing about moving on?"

"No"

"It happens to you slowly as you grow. You discover more about who you are and what you want, and then you realize that you need to make changes. Letting go is merely arriving at a decision— no more allowing something from the past to influence your life today or cut down your inner sense of peace and welfare." She faced Charlie.

"Are you ready for that change?"

"I...I..."

"All you need to do is to relinquish the beliefs and mental attitudes that keep you from receiving the pleasure of the moment. The issue comes in discovering precisely what that means. We have so many notions that keep us from living in the present moment, from becoming content and peaceful inside. Charlie, why don't you stay a little longer?" Mrs. Dempsey was afraid Charlie would fall through recovery if she was on her own.

"I'm grateful for your love and care, Mrs. Dempsey, but I want to be on my own. I'll be fine, I promise."

Charlie insisted on moving, so Mrs. Dempsey and her husband helped Charlie pack and furnished her new home.

The blossoming butterfly was now on her own, on her own terms, not from an absent mother, nor from a failed relationship, on her own where no one could hurt her.

Charlie, never missed therapy or work. She spent the weekends with the Dempsey's, but the weeknights were cold and lonely. Charlie was slowly reminded of what nights were like growing up. The nights for Charlie as an adult were horrific. She could not sleep, so she ate to ease the sleepless nights. Charlie was slipping, slipping fast.

The average person would think Charlie was doing fine. Therapy seemed to be going well, yet she was plummeting downhill each day. Mrs. Dempsey was correct: Charlie was not ready to leave them or be on her own. Charlie needed therapy for a long time, a fact she wasn't ready to accept.

"How is it alone, Charlie? Mrs. Dempsey sat next to her on the front porch of their house.

"I'm doing fine, Mrs. Dempsey."

"Are you sure?" she said, looking into her eyes.

Charlie looked down and began to cry. It wasn't easy; the nights were lonely and cold. The memories came back every day to haunt her, to remind her of who she was and where she came from.

"It's okay, Charlie. I understand you want to fight this battle, but you can't do it alone. You can learn from your history, but you can't live in it."

"How? It's hard to get these memories out of my mind."

"You can clutch the past so tightly to your chest that it leaves your arms too full to embrace the present. Sometimes we avoid experiencing where we are because we have developed a belief based on past experiences.

"It's too hard, Mrs. Dempsey."

"Moving on doesn't mean you completely forget the wonderful things from your past; it just means that you find a positive way of surviving without them in your present. You own every minute that you pass through. It is up to you to make the best use of each of them."

Mrs. Dempsey saw the change in Charlie, the good and the bad, and convinced her to move back to the Dempsey home. They sublet the apartment and explained to Charlie that her mental health was at stake. It was important to get the help she desperately needed. They agreed on a year to help Charlie, but after six months and then she was ready to move again.

"I need to be on my own, Mrs. Dempsey," she said. She wanted to fight the battles alone and try to face those wicked demons, the demons that haunted her for so many years. Charlie was consumed with being on her own. She blamed herself for not progressing. She was in a mood of rage most of the time. She stayed to herself, with no friends or co-workers.

However, she sparked the interest of Tommie, a co-worker at the all-girls school. He was working as a mentoring coach for at-risk kids. They talked primarily on a hi and bye basis until Charlie opened up to him during lunch one day when she was sitting alone.

"May I?" She heard the voice quietly say to her. She looked up and saw him smile.

"Sure, take a seat," she said as she moved her bag over for him to sit down.

"I'm Tommie."

"I'm Charlie. I know you."

"Yeah, I guess I'm somewhat popular around here." he chuckled.

"Hehe, you are, I guess."

"Why are you here, if I may ask."

Charlie sighed and looked at the sky. "I am a broken vessel and a disguised soul. Disguised under the image of being okay, but I am not. I carry a weight that is too much for me to bear, which I have been carrying from childhood." She paused, sniffed, then continued, "I was born to unloving parents, a mother who never even cared about me and a father I don't know. My troubles began when she brought home a man who was supposed to be my stepfather, but he brought along his devilish and evil children who tormented my life for several years. The one friend I had left me when I was helpless, weak and hurt."

Tommie listened and empathized with her, a bit surprised that she shared so much so quickly. He seemed to understand her life and her trials.

"My past isn't super smooth either," he started. "There were lots of emotional scars. So perhaps I am a broken vessel too that is being molded back into shape.

They talked many days together and would sometimes meet after work to share laughs, heartaches, and testimonies. The closer they became, the more Charlie trusted him and respected their friendship. They were both patient with each other, and the Dempsey's loved their friendship.

Tommie wasn't the average male. He did not date much or have many female friends. Some thought he was into men because they barely saw him with any woman as a friend or acquaintance. He was really reserved and careful about who he dated and trusted. Tommie confided in Charlie, telling her the secrets about him that he'd buried inside for many years. Charlie shared the most dreadful part about life, the sexual abuse and rape, and she was very detailed about how it happened. Although she was sexually abused by her stepsister and neighbors, the rape was the most tragic act for her. When she described the rape, he consoled her and cried with her. She went into detail about her tumultuous relationship with her mom, and he listened with deep concern.

Tommie opened up about his trials with his dad and the worst break-up of his life. Tommie painted the picture of his childhood and his first love while in college. They met in his freshman year of college and shared the same love for science. He was immediately smitten when he met her in the library on campus.

They started as friends and soon became more intimate. That was his first time with a woman. Tommie was in love from the beginning, but she was not sure about Tommie. However, she did like the attention he gave her. He was thinking long-term, while she was thinking temporary.

Tommie graphically explained to Charlie the night his heart was shredded to pieces. He'd gone to a college party alone, thinking his love went home to visit her parents for the weekend. To his surprise, she was at the party among a group of frat brothers heading towards a bedroom. He followed her to see what was happening. Tommie witnessed his first love sliding her sinuous tongue down the body of another man, not one but two, then joining them was her best friend. Tommie was crushed. She never knew he stood afar watching and crying as she moaned and screamed with passion.

Tommie slowly walked away and never looked back. His first love broke his heart and used him for his kindness. He didn't think love was supposed to be like that, he envisioned love to be perfect and everlasting.

Charlie and Tommie spent the rest of the time holding one another. It was then that they connected on a spiritual level. Charlie wondered who this man was, who this incredibly sensitive man was. He was like a God-sent angel to her, to guide and protect her.

Thomas Whittaker

C harlie and Tommie were hanging out strong for a few months; he was completely in touch with Charlie. They never identified what they were to each other. As far as anyone knew, they were great friends without the benefits. They both decided to wait to be intimate with one another until they were sure about the relationship. He understood her mentally and spiritually, and he had patience with her.

Tommie had a rough past. He was the oldest of nine children, the golden child, and excelled at everything he tried. He wanted to be the best for his brothers and sisters, a role model, so he made sure to accomplish what he started no matter what it took. His parents never asked him to do these things; he somehow thought that was what he needed to do.

Tommie's parents were an average couple, high school sweethearts who married right out of high school. His mom was a career homemaker. His dad secured a job with one of the local factories. They were very well situated as parents; his mom made sure the kids were taken care of, well-groomed and respectable. His dad worked 14 hours a day and was stern but fair. He had a level of respect in the community as a well-known preacher's kid. Tommie did not know that side of his dad; they did not go to church much, yet he knew his grandfather was a pastor. Tommie's parents wanted their children to establish themselves spiritually on their own terms. They only attended church when they deemed it necessary, you know, Mother's Day, Easter, Christmas, and an occasional New Year's Eve service.

Tommie's dad did not spend much time with the family, only for show and tell. He was there when it was time to make an appearance. A church service, a dinner party, that sort of thing. Tommie's mom handled everything from the kids to the bills; his dad provided the funds and nothing more. Tommie's dad was a rolling stone, to say the least. Not only did he have a herd of kids with Tommie's mom, he had another family with a woman he wasn't married to, but they shared five kids. Tommie was the oldest son of his mom and dad, but he had other brothers and sisters he never met. Tommie was old enough to know of his father's infidelity, which led him to think he had to be the man of the house. He had to be strong for his siblings and especially for his mother. Tommie did not have much of a relationship with his father. As Charlie co-existed with her mom, so did he co-exist with his dad.

Tommie was sixteen when he found out about his dad's adulterous ways. It was late in the evening when Tommie's dad returned home from one of his normal visits with the other family. Tommie's mom was furious that her husband was gone all day and much of the evening. He would normally respect the house and come home after work. But this night was different; Tommie's mom knew of the other woman and the distant family. She told him earlier on to make sure his wife and kids came before the gutter trash. She accepted his ways, his faults, and his shortcomings, but this night she had enough, and she needed to vent about his continued disrespect.

He walked through the door, and she started to yell at the top of her lungs. Tommie heard everything. His mom called him out about his mistress. His mom wanted his dad, Clarence to leave the other woman and finally be the man he promised to be. He argued that it was for the kids, and he had to go see his children. That's when Tommie's mom went into a rage!

"You don't tend to your children with me! What gives you the right to go see those bastard children?"

"But... they are my kids."

"Did I birth dogs for you?"

"You don't understand," he tried to explain.

" I forbid you from going to her even if it is for the kids."

Tommie heard his dad say, "Yes, ma'am." And they went on as if nothing happened.

Clarence went to work and came straight home afterwards. He was miserable not being able to see all of his children. Tommie grew angry with his dad for not respecting his mother, who worked so hard for the family.

Tommie's dad was visible but not really present. He did not attend sporting events for his brothers and sisters nor award ceremonies. Yet, his mother wanted a man in the house to provide for the family.

At sixteen, Tommie got his first job while going to school. He worked at the local funeral home. That seemed to excite him. He worked closely with the embalmer at the funeral home. He provided for his siblings when he could. The siblings looked up to their brother for guidance. Tommie had to grow up to be a man, in charge of the house without knowing exactly how that was supposed to look like.

He grew to love the human body and mind, and he soon joined the science club at school. However, he did anything to stay away from his dad. Gone most of the time, he saw his dad in passing, but there were no dad-son conversations.

Tommie was determined to excel despite his circumstances. He wanted to prove to his dad that it is possible to be a provider who shows love and support.

Tommie worked his way to an offer for a full-time position after high school, but Tommie had bigger goals. He wanted to become a doctor, to help people and provide a better life for them.

After graduating from high school with honors and landing a full scholarship to Tampa University with a major in biology, it was in college when Tommie began to face his demons of an absentee father. He began to drink his way through his problems, although he still excelled in college. He was naturally gifted with intelligence, yet he lacked self-esteem. The more Tommie hung around the frats at school, the more he became withdrawn. He talked to his mom daily, but his dad did not want anything to do with him.

Tommie did not visit home much in an effort to avoid his dad. He would meet his mom and siblings out; his mom was proud of him.

Drunk much of the time, Tommie was eager to keep going. He focused and realized he could not escape his pain with booze. He joined a future doctor's organization for black males. Intrigued by the support of others in the organization, he found other black males who had the same interests as him. They volunteered at local hospitals as a part of their club requirements. Tommie enjoyed volunteering, and that was where he found his passion for youth. He would spend time reading with the kids and talking with them. He found his true life's work in working with young people, especially young males.

During his sophomore year, Tommie changed his major to Psychology with a minor in Child Development. He wanted to help children who were suffering from childhood traumas. He eventually landed an internship at the Coastal Florida Mental Health Center, helping youth with trauma.

At graduation, his mom was there cheering him on. Clarence was nowhere in sight, but that wasn't new.

Tommie was moving forward with his life regardless of his failed relationship with his dad. Things seemed to be going well until his dad died of a heart attack, then he had to move back home to support his mom while taking classes online. He spent all his time with his mom, blocked out all the past, and focused on his mother. His mom, work, and school were his life and top priorities.

Once Tommie completed graduate school, his mom moved to Atlanta, Georgia, with the new love of her life. Tommie stayed in Florida, soon met Mrs. Dempsey at an employee conference, and they hit it off and remained friends. She was recruiting for her new school and knew he would be a perfect fit as a psychiatrist for the all-girls school. He was relatable and understating, and most importantly, he was kind. Thomas Whitaker was on track for a bright future with a promising career that he loved.

He was broken after all, too, but he faced all his demons. He didn't hide from them. The responsibility he shouldered at a young age of taking care of his family in his father's absence was a great deal to handle, but Tommie managed to cope with it all.

Tommie and Charlie

Tommie and Charlie spent more and more time together and continued to grow in their friendship. But Tommie wanted to ask Charlie to be more than just friends.

"Do you have plans tonight?" he asked while they were on their usual walk.

"Not really, I just want to do a few things around the house, but it's okay. I can do them later."

"Okay, would you like to go on a date with me?"

Charlie left his hand and turned to look at him. She watched his expression before smiling at him. "Yes."

He set the mood just right. He'd had asked her out on an official date, and he arranged for her to arrive by limo. She was in awe of the surprise and the effort he went to for her. Before Tommie, she'd never had anyone make her feel so special. For the first time, she was open about her past, and he accepted her for who she was. He did not care about the rape or the trauma. He only had her best interest at heart.

When Charlie arrived to the restaurant, the Dempsey's were there, some friends from the school, and to her surprise, her mom was there. Tommie wanted her mom to witness their happiness. You would think he was proposing, but he only wanted to date her. Tommie wanted the women in his life to feel important. He did not want Charlie or anyone to be treated like his dad treated his mom. He loved Charlie as she was, even though she was a bit scarred, he appreciated her genuine innocence. He wanted to go all out for her; he wanted to prove that she could trust him with her heart. He wanted to show her that he was going to love her and cherish her not because she was vulnerable and weak but because he loved her for who she was. The mood was set, and her favorite song, "A song for You" by Donny Hathaway, was playing in the background. Tommie wanted to make a lasting impression.

As the evening progressed, Tommie met Charlie at the door with his hand out to greet her, presenting her with a single red rose.

"For you, madam," he said to her as they both laughed. Tommie led the way with everyone holding hands in a circle. Charlie and Tommie were positioned in the middle of the circle, a circle of togetherness, a bond with friends and family. Tommie looked at Charlie with love in his eyes and asked, "Will you take my heart and cherish it from this day until forever? I want to slowly take the time to understand your mind and soul, understand what makes you smile and what makes you sad. My promise to you will be to love you. Will you be my girlfriend, Charlie?"

Charlie was dazed and looked in his eyes, something she never did. Gazing into Tommie's eyes, she accepted his promise. She softly whispered in his ear, "Yes, I will."

His heart leaped for joy. He gave her a kiss on the cheek and hugged her. Then, they celebrated the night away with friends and family.

When Charlie and her mom went off by themselves, there was an awkward silence between them. Dorothy couldn't look Charlie in the eye. Charlie wanted to know why her mom decided to come to experience her happiness. She had a lot of questions for Dorothy.

"Why did you hate me?"

Dorothy was quiet. She tried hard to fight the tears that were welling up in her eyes, but she couldn't. They fell freely from her face.

"What did I do to deserve all the hate and neglect you showed me? The abuse and the lack of care you gave me. You were absent all of my life, never for once asking how I was or even try to talk to me. On days when I was sick, I took care of myself, even though I was a little girl. Why did you do all these things to me?"

Dorothy looked at her daughter, she had no right to punish Charlie like that, but she was not ready to be responsible for anyone but herself.

"I resented you for being born. You were the memory of a man who walked out like a coward, no explanation or a goodbye. In a sense, you ruined my life of enjoyment. I always imagined him staying if you weren't born. I am truly sorry for the hurt I have caused."

"You, my dear, are the coward! Your selfish intentions caused me a life of grief and hardship. You could not get over a man who left you; little did you realize you left as well. So, you hated me for his mistake. You are worse than I thought. Why are you even here? You could care less about my happiness! After all, you never cared right from the beginning."

"This is my sincere apology. I made things worse for you, but I am here to mend the shattered pieces of our relationship. I haven't been a good mother, and I know that, but I want and to see the glow you have. We can talk about this later. It's your night to shine."

They had a small breakthrough. Dorothy thought it would be best to stay in Florida for a few months after she was retired, allowing her and Charlie to work on mending their relationship.

They began going to therapy together, having lunch, and spending much-needed time together. Tommie sometimes went to therapy with them; things were getting better with her mom. Dorothy was glad for Charlie, and she respected Tommie for accepting Charlie as wounded as she was.

When it was time for Dorothy to head back to North Carolina, Charlie and her mom were on to a new journey in life. Dorothy headed back to North Carolina only to return a few months later. Finally, Charlie and Dorothy thought it would be best if she moved to Florida to live permanently as a family.

Tommie and Charlie were growing in love together. Charlie was doing great, accepting the love Tommie freely gave, and she cherished every bit of it. Charlie finished her academic pursuit in the medical field as an administrative medical assistant. She also received an offer to work in the office with one of the parents from the girl's school. They took Charlie on temporarily, and she loved the work. She really excelled at the job. She had the best boyfriend, a new career, and a new relationship with her mom. Charlie finally realized that she could be happy.

"How do you feel today, Charlie?" her therapist asked.

"I feel good, Charlie" she smiled.

"Have you noticed any changes these days?"

"Yes, I have."

"That's wonderful. What changes do you notice?"

"I feel happy," she said, smiling again.

"Why do you feel happy?"

"I... "Charlie stopped.

"Go on," the therapist said calmly.

"I feel I have hope, hope to live for each day."

"What motivates that hope?"

"I now have something to live for. And someone, too, there is no holding back now. I want to face all my demons now and overcome them!"

"That's great, Charlie. I am so proud of you. I want you to know that you have to be positive and live each day with the notion that you are going to do something incredible. I'm glad you have let go of the past, forgiving those who hurt you so you can move on and believe in yourself."

"Thank you very much for not giving up on me."

"You did not give up on yourself either," the therapist smiled.

Initially, Charlie thought it was all a dream, always waiting for destruction to happen. Tommie assured her this was real, that he was real, and that she deserved happiness. He wanted Charlie to know she meant the world to him.

They both decided to start attending church. They needed more to guide them in the spiritual aspect of life. The two of them joined church together, prayed together, and attended therapy together and separately.

Unfortunately, things went downhill for them when Tommie's mom got sick; she was diagnosed with a brain tumor. Tommie was having a hard time with his mom's illness; this was time for Charlie to console Tommie. But, was she mentally prepared to be there for someone and maintain her own sanity?

Charlie would greet Tommie with a smile when they saw each other, which was much less with his mom being sick. Charlie never thought she would ever be able to truly comfort the man she adored, even though she was trying so hard to be strong for him.

"It's gonna be fine Tommie, everything is going to be okay. I know it."

"Are you sure?" Tommie sat head down as Charlie put an arm around his shoulders.

"Yes, I believe God, and I know he has a reason for all of this. I just want you to be hopeful and positive. Things are going to be okay." She hugged him and patted him on the back.

She was scared but tried not to show it to him. She knew he would be worried, and this wasn't the time for her to cause him any worry.

As Tommie was losing his mom, he was gaining the best thing that ever happened to him. His relationship with Charlie flourished into a more intimate one, having a magical night of consensual bonding of bodies. He held her body tight and slow, caressing every inch of her with concern and respect. Tommie explored her body as a fresh new butterfly that bloomed from a scattered caterpillar. Charlie disappeared into another world she did not want to come back from. He made all the past awful sexual abuse, the rape, and her first boyfriend disappear from her mind.

She was falling in love and was nervous at the same time. She had no idea Tommie was falling in love as well as he connected his body with hers. The night was unforgettable. Charlie wondering if it was all true, Tommie held her close. He wanted Charlie to be there to the end. All she could do was believe him even though she had hesitations.

They awakened from a night of passion, and Tommie received a phone call from his sister, the call that ended it all. His mom had passed away. Charlie took his hand and consoled him, prayed and cried.

"It's gonna be fine Tommie, she has gone to rest in the bosom of the Lord," she whispered to him. She had to be stronger for him. His mother was the reason he carried on this far, and now she was gone.

It was a Saturday morning. They drove to his mom's house to say his final goodbye. When he arrived, a flash of repressed memories of his dad and mom in a web of infidelity occupied his mind. He held back the anger and started to cry uncontrollably. Tommie released the pain and laid his head on his mom's heart when they viewed her body. He stayed there as the tears rolled down his face.

Charlie was there every step of the way; she did not let him leave her side.

The day would come when he laid his mom to rest. Charlie beside him, he said goodbye to his mom on this side of heaven. At the repass, Tommie felt more bonded with Charlie, as if his mom was giving him a sign. He knew he needed to make Charlie a part of his life forever. It didn't matter where they were; Tommie knew he loved her with all his heart. So, he figured it was the perfect time to ask her to marry him, burying a part of his heart and replacing it with a new one. He was going to pop the question right there in front of his family and siblings. Nothing was planned or rehearsed, but he could not let that moment slip away. She was everything he needed and wanted in a woman: supportive, loving, caring, understanding. Any quality you may wish to find in a woman, Charlie had them, and he wasn't going to make the mistake of letting her go.

Tommie was looking for Charlie. She was gathering herself in the restroom. The emotions from his mom's passing caught up with her. She hid from Tommie to grieve privately. As she came out of the restroom refreshed,

Tommie grabbed Charlie by the hand. "Charlie, you gave oxygen to a breathless lung, you brought sunshine to a cloudy day, you opened my mind to endless possibilities and most importantly you loved me when others would not have. Charlie, will you become my wife, my partner, my soulmate, and my best friend forever?"

Charlie's heart was fluttering and her hand was shaking like a leaf with a river flowing from her eyes. She happily accepted his proposal. "Yes, I will be honored to be your wife and everlasting lover for life." They embraced each other. It was as though the caterpillar was blossoming into a beautiful butterfly. Their love was endless and was meant to be. At that moment, they shared a bittersweet peace, reminiscing of all that brought them to this day.

The days ahead for Charlie and Tommy were not going to be easy; Tommie knew it was time for him to go to counseling on his own. They both agreed they'd do sessions alone and together before setting a wedding date.

Tommie was traveling a lot more to visit his siblings since his mom's death. He wanted to be the anchor for his family since everyone now looked to him as their backbone.

He was living his childhood over again as an adult. Only this time, he was more mature. Charlie would often travel with him, spending most of her time studying; Tommie wanted her to stay focused on her goals. That was what she loved about Tommie: he allowed her to make decisions for herself, and he supported her.

With Dempsey's help, Charlie started making plans to move into her own place. Tommie was not too happy with Charlie moving alone, so he asked her to move in with him. Apprehensive at first, she took the leap of faith to move in with Tommie. The best decision they made together. The closer they got with one another, the more Charlie was finally assured that they were always going to be together. She thought it would be a great idea to set a date for the wedding. Being together for over a year, they shared their most secret thoughts.

The date was set for New Year's Eve, and the plans were being made. They would have a small, intimate wedding with family and friends, around 50 people.

They announced the date to everyone; the pre-wedding engagement party was planned for Thanksgiving weekend. The couple planned a huge dinner party to celebrate.

Tommie had a beautiful home that sat on the lake, and it had enough room for everyone to join them. Charlie made sure she arranged the perfect dinner to share their love with the people closest to them. As time drew near, the house was transformed into a picture from a movie scene.

Everyone was having a good time, laughing and making memories. Tommie drifted away for a while. Charlie noticed his posture change. He was missing his mom. Charlie went to wrap her body around his, giving him the attention he needed; they always seemed to know how to comfort each other. Tommie gathered himself and rejoined the celebration. She was always there for him, assuring him each day that he wasn't alone in the journey.

The night ended with a dance contest and another news alert: Charlie was pregnant. You could see the gleam on Tommie's face. Nothing could break them apart now.

They celebrated the new life that was about to be a part of their world, and they were one month away from their wedding day. Everything was going well for them. Charlie had been promoted on her job, and they were attending church and were looking forward to serving as the new couple's ministry liaisons. Life could not get better for Tommie and Charlie.

The countdown has started. Tommie and Charlie will soon become one. They completed all the right measures to assure they would have an understanding marriage with pre-marital counseling weekly.

Charlie was working through her abandonment issues. She trusted Tommie with all her heart. He never gave any indication he would leave her. Charlie loved Tommie regardless of any misunderstandings they had, which were rare because they learned to pray through any trials. He would go to every doctor visit with her and make sure she was cared for in all aspects of life. Charlie did not have to worry about anything. The brokenness carried for so many years as a victim was transformed into a vessel to help others.

Together the couple started a non-profit organization for battered children, both boys and girls. Charlie wanted all girls, but Tommie knew there were boys that needed healing as well. It was a program the kids entered in fourth grade and would continue to high school.

"Alright now, boys, let's listen." The boys scurried back to their seats and listened attentively to what Tommie was about to say. They admired him, he was a good listener and coach. He understood the kids; they were always open to tell him anything they were facing. "What did we learn about ourselves and our past?"

"Make peace with it!" they chorused

"That's right. No matter what happens, no matter the outcome,"

"You're going to be just fine!"

"Who alone has the power to change things or change the way you think about things?"

"I do!"

"Yes, that's it, kids. There is something very powerful and liberating about surrendering to change and embracing it. This is where personal growth and evolution reside."

"But," a chestnut-brown haired boy with big, rimless glasses stood up.

"What is it, Henry?"

"These changes are hard to make. There are lots of people who hurt us, so how do we change that fact when it has already happened?"

"That is why there are new opportunities waiting out there for you. Nobody gets through life without losing someone they love, or something they need, or something they thought was meant to be. But it is these losses that make us stronger and eventually move us towards future opportunities. See the times of hurt and all you face as a learning phase. A phase for you to appreciate every good thing that happens to you, either big or small. A phrase for you to let this change happen, you have to learn about yourself because the change begins with you first."

"Oh, I understand now."

"Yes, Henry. There is no better way to build self-confidence than to have faith in yourself."

Tommie was great at mentoring the boys. He and Charlie enjoyed working together with the kids. The program offered free meals also. Charlie worked primarily with young kids who were victims of rape and sexual abuse.

She wanted to be a pillar of hope to other young, weak girls who were broken like she was.

"Believe in yourself," Charlie began a talk with the kids that day. "That is the message that we encounter constantly. In books, Tv shows, superhero comic books, myths and legends. They tell us that we can accomplish anything if we believe in ourselves."

"But we cannot accomplish anything in the world simply through belief. If it were that easy, I would be soaring in the sky right now," a kid scoffed, and the rest burst out laughing.

"Yes, but believing in yourself and accepting yourself for who you are is an important factor in success, and that self-esteem plays an important role in living a flourishing life" Charlie smiled. "It provides us with belief in our abilities and the motivation to carry them out, ultimately reaching fulfillment as we navigate life with a positive outlook. So, that is why self-esteem has a direct relationship with our overall well-being."

"Is self-esteem the same as self-confidence?"

"Great question, Emily. Self-esteem is not self-confidence; self-confidence is about your trust in yourself and your ability to deal with challenges, solve problems and engage successfully with the world. Self-esteem is what we think, feel, and believe about ourselves."

Life hadn't been fair and loving to her growing up, but she wanted to serve as an excellent example of self-love to other people. So, she diligently took care of the children and talked to them often.

As the days get closer to the big day, Charlie was nervous about what was about to happen, even though Tommie assured her he would make sure he would be the best husband, father, and friend. Pre-marital counseling helped her, but her fears of her past would sneak in and make her doubt.

The BIG Day

It was a week before the wedding, and Tommie and Charlie both had the butterflies of anticipation. Tommie had a long day planned for Charlie the day before the wedding. He scheduled her a spa day so she could be pampered. Her appointment was for the works. She was to be pampered all day with no interruptions. Charlie was overjoyed with excitement and finally let go of the doubts about Tommie.

As Charlie was prepping for her day of pampering, Tommie was linking up with some of his frat brothers who came in town for the wedding. As they said their goodbyes, Tommie and Charlie cried and prayed then went their separate ways. Mrs. Dempsey went with Charlie out for the pamper day, and Charlie's few friends were unable to attend the day of festivities, so Mrs. Dempsey took one for the team. Charlie was impressed with everything Tommie did for her, from the personal driver to meals at five-star restaurants. Tommie went all out for his wife-to-be. Little did Charlie know her friends were there waiting to surprise her for the greatest bachelorette party. The party bus was loaded with all the things a girl wanted.

Dorothy was sitting in the back of the bus with nonalcoholic champagne. They popped bottles and screamed out. "It's a party!!!!" The first stop was manis, pedis and a much-needed massage. The ladies indulged in exotic fruit and chocolates at the spa. As they began to wrap up, a tall, dark chocolate stripper came thrusting in the door; he ripped off his pants. I think Mrs. Dempsey fainted in awe of his well-endowed package. Dorothy was enjoying every single minute of it. The reserved Charlie was trying to hold herself together, but she finally let go and joined the fun. The show lasted 30 minutes, then they left to get a meal which Tommie planned. The dinner was the icing on the cake. Through laughs and tears, Mrs. Dempsey and Dorothy, were becoming great friends. As the evening ended, they went to their hotel suite at the Ritz Carlton filled with roses and champagne, compliments of Tommie. The ladies sat around telling stories and having conversations about the new life of Charlie and Tommie.

Tommie was out with his fellas; he was not into the strip club scene, so they spent most of the day chatting it up at a cigar lounge. They started the day with an afternoon round of golf, cleaned up at the Marriott and had a shot of Crown Royal. Although Tommie did not want to go to the strip club, he did not say strippers could not come to him.

Suddenly, there was a knock on the door. Tommie's friends told him to get the door. They'd ordered some appetizers before going to the cigar bar. Tommie opened the door, and to his surprise, a tall, almond blond-hair female with nothing on but a sarong and lingerie was smiling at him.

"Man, I told y'all I did not want strippers, but if you insist." He invited Almond Joy into the room. The shots kept coming, and Almond Joy was giving Tommie the lap dance of his life. He was mesmerized by her skill of the special touch. She rubbed her body against his until he opened his eyes of lust. He pushed her away gently and asked her to leave. He paid her over what she was offered, and she left. His boys were upset that he just let her go.

"Man, what is wrong with you? She was giving you a roller coaster ride."

"I can't do Charlie like that. She would be devastated if she found out. Also, you remember what happened in college with Sidney?" They all looked at each other and silently agreed that it was time to head to the cigar bar. Tommie couldn't bear to cheat on her. He had vowed never to break her heart or bring back the old, ugly memories to her. She didn't deserve that. He loved her too much.

They all put on their Sunday best and headed out for a boy's night out. They were chatting it up in the car, then a loud screeching sound came from the back of the car. One of his friends was on the passenger side of the car could barely see, but he saw enough to know Tommie was in the worse shape of them all. On the way to the cigar bar, they were in a terrible car accident. A driver hit them from the back where Tommie was sitting in the car. The impact was so hard that the other car was stuck to the trunk of the car Tommie was in.

The glass cup fell from Charlie's hand immediately. She felt cold, there was no rain. The weather was warm outside. This was a sign, but she didn't know what it was.

"Somebody dial 911," the voice echoed.

"There's been an accident… yes…" the woman standing hurriedly made the call.

Tommie was in so much pain, it was unbearable. He wanted to give in to the darkness overwhelming him, to let go of everything. Anything was better than the pain he was passing through, then slowly, his eyes closed. They had a hard time retrieving his almost lifeless body. There was blood flowing everywhere, and he was barely clinging on to dear life.

He was rushed to the hospital, weak from losing too much blood. Tommie's thoughts were emerging, not now when he was to marry the love of his life. If anything happened to him, Charlie would never recover, and he would never forgive himself for leaving her in this world alone and even more broken. She was doing so well; this tragedy would kill her. Tommie was trying to hold on. He wanted to be there for Charlie until the end of time as he had promised her.

"You can survive it, Tommie," he told himself quietly. "You have to live for yourself and Charlie. You don't want to see her sad forever, so you have to live no matter what."

At the hospital, he was immediately rushed into the ICU. The doctors noticed he had a large cut on the side of his forehead, so he was taken to surgery. He also had injuries to his left leg, bruises, and cuts nearly all over his body. Tommie was about to go through the hardest part of life.

He was in surgery for six hours. The gash on the side of his forehead was from glass and fiber that was embedded in his skull. His leg was broken, yet he survived the surgery. Unable to speak for himself, he was lying there alive yet dead in spirit.

His family finally arrived; they were able to contact them by his identification in his wallet. Charlie was nowhere in sight, but the nurses arranged for Tommie to have minimal cell phone usage. His friends in the car with him all went to the same hospital, but Tommie suffered the most injuries.

Everyone was frantically trying to reach Charlie. When she didn't answer her phone after 12 tries, they got in touch with Mr. Dempsey. He went to the hotel where they were and quickly asked to see Charlie alone. As he gave Charlie the news, the tears rolled down her face, and her body fell weak. She was speechless and withdrawn from everything around her. Mrs. Dempsey helped her to the car.

Charlie's thoughts mirrored Tommie's. "The love of my life, my hero, my lifeline, he could not be hurt. He cannot leave me this way." When they arrived at the hospital, Charlie was weak and shaking, unprepared for what was to come.

Charlie was escorted to Tommie's room. He was attached to a ventilator with tubes everywhere. "My life is over, our baby, our life is nonexistent." She reflected on the memories, the good times, and how much she enjoyed Tommie. Then, leaning over to Tommie's ear, and whispered softly, "I know you cannot speak, but I know you can hear me. We will get through this, and you cannot leave me now. You cannot leave us." She took his hand, held her head on his chest, and uttered, "You are the vessel I needed in my life." She was going to try to be strong for him, although she couldn't watch him as he was. He was in pain, and there was nothing she could do about it. She hated that.

After she left his room, Charlie's thoughts were scattered. Why did this happen to me? Why do bad things always happen to me? Charlie was looking like a ghost glaring on outside the window of the waiting room. She paused in shock. Tommie was not there to hold her. Their wedding was less than 22 hours away. Charlie fell to the ground in disbelief. The nurses moved Charlie to another room where she was given a few tests to make sure the baby was alright. Her anxiety had gotten the best of her. She rested for a short time to calm her nerves. Charlie could not accept this harsh reality of life.

Mrs. Dempsey stayed with Charlie. Tommie's sister contacted everyone to notify them that the wedding was postponed. Those in town were welcome to stop by the hospital to visit Charlie. There were restricted visitors for Tommie.

Charlie was up and moving around, but she refused to leave the hospital. She wanted to remain at the hospital until she was able to hear Tommie's voice. As Charlie sat there still in another world, she held his hand, talked to him, and caressed him. When Dorothy arrived, she simply held Charlie, and they cried together.

"Charlie"

"Mom," Charlie hugged her mom and cried. She needed someone she could cry to.

"I know baby. I don't know how, but it's going to be alright.

Healing Grace

Dorothy never left Charlie's side. They tried to get Charlie to leave the hospital for a break, but she wouldn't budge. They had to force her to eat, reminding her to keep the baby healthy. Once her blood pressure became extremely high, she was ordered to leave in order to keep the baby alive. The stress she was carrying was putting stress on the baby. Charlie did not go far, though. She sat up in the lobby. When Tommie woke up, she needed to be there; he needed her, and she was ready to give him everything he wanted.

Charlie was deeply saddened by the sudden changes in her life. She wanted to be strong for Tommie, yet deep down, she was hurting, trying to make the best of a bad situation.

Dorothy and Mrs. Dempsey took turns staying with both Charlie and Tommie. Still, they did not notice that Charlie was slipping into depression. Charlie was placed on bed rest due to the anxiety attacks she was having as well as her up and down blood pressure.

At home, her mind was idle. She asked for the therapist to come to her, and she agreed. Charlie would get visits from her twice a week; her therapist noticed the change in Charlie's behavior. Of course, with everything that had happened, Charlie would naturally have a decline in progress. She was not ready to handle this life occurrence on her own. The therapist offered to see Charlie four times a week. She was mostly there with Charlie to comfort her. She became an aide to Charlie because she did not want Charlie to go down a spiral slope of bitterness and regret.

Tommie was not getting any better, but still fighting to live for himself but, most importantly, for Charlie. He promised to love her unconditionally forever. Why would this happen? Was this is a test of their faith? It was more than what they could bear. Was this a test of endurance for them?

With the same thoughts in his mind, Tommie was slowly opening his eyes. There was some brain activity, and he was coming around. Mrs. Dempsey was there with him, and she quickly ran to get help. Several doctors and nurses came running to see this miracle.

As Tommie was coming around, his eyes were glazed. He kept looking around like he didn't know where he was. The doctor ran a test checked his heart rate, and checked his X-rays. Tommie was alive and breathing on his own after three days in a coma. He wasn't entirely coherent, yet his family was called in to hear the good news. When Charlie got the call that Tommie was out of the coma, she wanted to be at his side for a moment. Charlie managed to convince her therapist and her mom to take her to the hospital.

Charlie couldn't wait to see Tommie. It was like she was meeting him for the first time. She fell to his side with a sigh of relief.

Tommie still had a long way to go, but that didn't matter to Charlie. She was thankful that he was alive. His eyes gave a flash of light. A tear rolled from his bruised face. His love, his life partner, was enough for him to keep up the fight. Charlie stayed with Tommie for what seemed like hours.

Tommie was in the hospital for a month then went to rehab for recovery. He was learning to speak again. There was very little mobility because he had to walk with an artificial leg. They were able to remove the glass from his skull so that it did not cause damage to his brain, but there was significant damage to his legs. He only saw Charlie a few times in recovery and once at the hospital. She had to remain on bed rest, so they communicated through Skype most of the time.

Tommie had a while before he could go home, and Charlie was getting anxious about his arrival. Tommie was still fighting and was on a long road of hurtful nights and days. Rehab was slow, and Tommie was trying to rush things along. The more he tried to push himself, the less he progressed. After another month passed by, and Tommie was still having a hard time getting around. It was difficult to adjust to his new leg and life.

The old Tommie was full of optimism, but the new Tommie couldn't get past this depressive stage. He was away from Charlie, and his family only came once a week if that. He couldn't speak clearly, so Charlie would try to reach out some days, and he would make excuses not to talk to her.

One day after few weeks of therapy, Tommie looked up and thought his mind was playing tricks on him. He thought he saw Sidney, his first girlfriend, walking down the hallway. He wasn't crazy; it was her.

He held out his hand to touch hers, and he started to weep. They sat for a moment in silence. Tommie felt perplexed. All he could do was think of Charlie, but his first love was there as a sign of hope. Why was she here, after all this time? She came to see him, to get him through rehab and recovery. Sidney looked into Tommie's eyes and said, "It was fate that brought me to you. I regretted the day I broke your heart, and I'd do anything to make it up to you."

He respectfully and slowly gave her a kind smile. Tommie mouthed the word, go, and pointed his frail finger toward the door.

"I am not leaving until I get what I came for. Tommie, I messed up bad, but you were not innocent in this breakup either. You came there to the frat party and saw me vulnerable and high, and you did nothing. I was ganged raped, one-by-one they inserted their private parts in me. I guess you thought I was having a good time, huh. At first, I was, but I was high out of my mind. I did not realize what was going on until I said STOP. You were not there to rescue me. I admit it; I was wrong for the drugs and partying, but the rape destroyed me. I had no choice but to run."

Tommie was trying hard to speak. "I am sorry, but I am engaged to be married." His voice was weak. "Why now, Sidney? It's been years. Why didn't you tell me about the drugs?"

"Wait a minute. You're engaged? Does your soon-to-be wife know the horrible things you have done? What if I put that bug in her ear? I said I came to get what I want. She is a non-factor to me. Why don't we give her a call?" Tommie used all the strength he had to tell her to get out and never come back.

Tommie was determined to heal for Charlie, and no one would change that. Especially not the ghost of the girlfriend from the past. The past came back to haunt him, that dreadful night of fear. His first love betrayed him. It was at that moment he realized he needed to get better for himself and tell Charlie who he really was. He requested to have a mental evaluation and get the real help he needed. It was time to face his fears and come to terms with the death of his dad. He never told Charlie or anyone his dad died of a heart attack at the mental hospital he was admitted to when he was in college. Tommie's dad suffered from mental illness all of his life and masked the illness with women and alcohol, which was carried down to Tommie. His dad showed signs of abuse early in Tommie's life shortly after Tommie's mom demanded that he stop seeing his other family.

While Tommie was at college, his dad was admitted to a mental hospital after he tried to kill Tommie's mother with a knife. His dad was out all day drinking and came home at 3AM. He attacked Tommie's mom for not cooking a meal for him. The only visible result was a knife wound on her face, but her life changed forever after that. She was left to take care of the kids while he was hospitalized. Tommie blamed himself for the incident; if he did not go to college, he would've been there for his mom to protect her from the beast. Tommie lived with this guilt for years; he adored his mother and would do anything for her. Anything.

Tommie needed to tell Charlie the truth, he needed to tell her there may be mental concerns for the baby, and he needed to deal with the guilt and old wounds. With the help of his therapist, he pinned a letter to Charlie. Mrs. Dempsey read the letter to Charlie while she was still on bed rest. Charlie was in utter disbelief; she could not understand why Tommie hid this from her.

We were open about everything. I opened my heart and confessed my innermost scars. Why didn't he do the same? Even though she didn't want to believe it, the letter answered all of her questions.

"I was afraid to tell you for fear of losing you. You were the first woman I was close since Sidney, and I could not lose the only person who saw me for me. You are my everything."

Charlie wrote a letter to Tommie and closed it with her innermost thoughts. "I wonder if you would have told me this if Sidney did not come to see you. Why did she have to make you tell me the truth? You should've been honest. You know you could have told me anything, and I would still love you. Tommie, you changed my life for the better. No one, not even Sidney, would make me leave you. Your past is what made you. Your present is what will create the new you."

They both needed to heal from their past life to have an extraordinary future.

Tommie and Charlie both agreed to get married there in the hospital before Tommy returned home, and they did just that. Dorothy rolled Charlie into the hospital chapel, puffy and bloated. Charlie was determined to make a commitment to Tommie. He met her with a gleam of joy. They confessed their love and were married, both stricken down in pain, they embraced for a moment. Life could only get better from here.

Tommie was still baffled by Sidney's response to wanting to be with him. He had just married the love of his life, but he could not get Sidney off his mind. Although he told Charlie the truth about his dad's mental illness, he did not tell her about everything. He swore never to tell anyone.

As Charlie got closer to her baby's due date, all was well with the Whittaker's. Charlie delivered a month early; thankfully, Tommie was able to witness the birth of their baby girl, Grace Taylor Whittaker. She came in with big, beautiful eyes and chubby cheeks weighing 5lbs and 6oz. Tommie was smitten from the beginning. He instantly fell in love with Grace, and he fell even more in love with Charlie.

Charlie was in the hospital for a week because she was having trouble with the swelling. Tommie did not leave her side. When they were finally able to go home with baby Grace, Dorothy and Charlie felt it would be good for Dorothy to move in permanently to help them as Tommie was still getting better. Hesitant at first, Tommie agreed with the arrangement. She wasn't the best mom to Charlie, but she was trying and proved herself to be a good person.

They definitely needed the assistance; Charlie wasn't working, so they were living off Tommie's savings and disability checks. However, they made the best of what they had and seemed to be adjusting just fine.

Sidney's Strikes Again

Tommie was getting stronger every day; he was Charlie's right arm aside from her mother. Grace was going on a month old. Charlie was up walking and feeling great. She was going back to work in a few weeks. Tommie would be a stay-at-home dad caring for Grace.

The couple moved into married life and parenthood with a breeze. Tommie was dealing with his drama on his own, regularly seeing a therapist for things he kept hidden for many years. Charlie supported him with his forthcoming mental illness, and Charlie was healing from her previous depression.

They wanted to work; they wanted a lifelong happy marriage. Tommie was also hiding his ex-girlfriend in his heart. She was still calling and texting, although he told her to stay away. She was persistent.

On what would have been an ordinary Thursday, Sidney showed up at their home. She searched and searched until she found out where he lived. Charlie opened the door to a surprise guest and went to get Tommie. His expression his lifeless. He was thinking, why did she come to my home to disrespect my family? What did this woman want?

She was introduced to Charlie as an old college friend, but Charlie knew it was more. Holding Grace in her arms, Charlie walked to the side of the room where the ex was standing and politely asked Sidney to leave her home. Sidney was determined to stay. She wanted to talk to Charlie privately. Tommie declined for her to speak to Charlie; there was nothing to say. What they had was in the past. As she stood there between Charlie and Tommie, she calmly explained to them she was Nikki's sister, and there was more. The family that adopted her moved to Florida. Charlie was stunned; Tommie was confused.

"Who is Nikki," Tommie asked.

"She used to be my best friend." Charlie tried to jog Tommie's memory with a few facts from the story she'd told him about Dwight.

Sidney tried to convince Charlie that she was, in fact, Nikki's sister, one of the many children Jackie gave up for adoption. But Charlie only knew of the siblings that Nikki lived with. The three convened in a private area of the home while Dorothy took baby Grace.

After the breakup, Sidney was in many abusive relationships and went to prison for a short time. In prison, she found out about her brothers and sisters and her birth mom, Jackie. Ironically, Nikki was in the same prison for selling drugs and attempted murder. Nikki was in prison for life; prison was her new home.

Sidney and Nikki got to know each other, and Sidney told Nikki about the man she let slip away because she was so messed up. She was determined to reach out to Tommie but didn't know how until she heard of the accident from one of their mutual friends. She was able to find Tommie through his brother. It was at the hospital when she visited Tommie that she learned he was with Charlie. She knew of Charlie from Nikki. Charlie was all Nikki talked about. She had pictures of them throughout the years. When Sidney walked into the hospital and saw pictures of him and Charlie, she recognized her sister's long-lost friend. Sidney looked at Tommie and Charlie with a hint of mischief in her eyes

"There is more we have been hiding from you, Charlie," Tommie interjected quickly.

"I think it is time for you to leave. You have said enough." Sidney attempted to continue, but Tommie kept stopping her, yelling at her.

Charlie needed to make sure Tommie did not explode; he was dealing with enough already. She squeezed Tommie's hand tightly. Charlie asked Sidney to talk with her privately. Sidney saw the hurt in Tommie's eyes and did not speak of the rape nor the real story of how Tommie's dad died. Tommie pacing the floor, wondering what they were saying. He knew it was time to say goodbye and get rid of the grief he was holding. Little did he know Charlie only had one question: where is Nikki?

Charlie was not ready to see Nikki and hoped Sidney did not tell her about her whereabouts. Charlie was not ready to open that Pandora's box. She thanked Sidney for the truthfulness and wished all the best, but it would not be wise to keep in touch. Sidney went on her way, said goodbye to Tommie, and walked away.

Tommie was bawled up in a knot, crying and weeping. Charlie was not sure what to do, why did this hurt him so badly. Was he still in love with Sidney? Was he feeling guilty for not knowing Sidney was a broken vessel as he was?

Charlie tried to softly whisper in his ear. Life has a funny way of turning travesty into victory. Charlie figured Sidney was sent in both of their lives to heal them and teach them.

"This isn't your fault; she could only save herself. This is only a test of your sanity. You've come too far to go downward."

Charlie spent the rest of the night holding him. Tommie was a mess. She had no choice but to let him admit to the demons that were haunting him to leave his body. This was something he needed to do on his own.

Tommie tossed and turned all night. Charlie remained by his side, not knowing what to do. She called Mrs. Dempsey; they came over and thought he needed treatment; his mental illness was grabbing him by threads. With serious thoughts, they agreed to have Tommie sent to a facility for 30 days. Tommie was trying to hold it together for everyone but himself.

Charlie began working again to provide for herself and her daughter. She knew she was ready to face any challenge that came her way. She and Dorothy continued to care for Grace.

A month went by quickly, and it was time for Tommie to come home. To her surprise, Tommie was a different person. He had lost weight, and he was very withdrawn. The medication and isolation made him into a walking zombie. Tommie tried his best to recover, and Charlie remained committed to him and his recovery.

Grace did not make him feel better; no one could bring him out of his own misery. He did not talk much nor wanted to be touched or bothered the first night home from the facility. He eventually went to sleep in the same clothing he wore from the hospital.

He refused to let Charlie console him, as if he blamed her for putting him away for a month. He was cold-hearted towards Charlie. She had no idea Tommie was on suicide watch for the first 15 days of his stay. Tommie forbade the facility staff to tell Charlie. He wanted his life to end.

On the following Friday morning, everything seemed normal. Tommie woke up playing with Grace, greeted Charlie with a hug, and went on with his daily routine of doing nothing. But it was different from the day before; another person arrived that Friday. It sure was not Tommie who came home in a dark daze. It was odd, to say the least.

Charlie assumed everything was going to be fine, so she went to work. Tommie, Dorothy, and Grace were at the house catching up on family time. Dorothy thought Tommie was a little off but figured he needed a day to get back to reality.

"Grace and I are headed out for part of the day, but we can stay with you if you would like."

"No, I need to have some time alone. After that, I will be just fine."

Tommie looked at the whole house from where he sat, then turned to the picture on the wall. Charlie was smiling brightly in the white gown she wore. He could see the glow in her eyes, a smile filled with hope and happiness. He loved her, but he couldn't bear to let her see him like this. He was drifting away, much faster than anybody imagined. He was very good at hiding his pain from everyone.

His condition could worsen at any time, and he could do something he would regret for the rest of his life, but he could not let Charlie see him in the pathetic state he was in. She had been through a lot in her life, and the thought of seeing her return back to that state made him sad.

He looked at the next picture of them with Grace. Oh, how he loved his little daughter; he remembered how he held her in his arms when she was given birth. The laughter of warmth she gave him, the innocent look of her eyes. But he wasn't going to be there to watch her grow or get to see her first steps. Or hear her say *'Dada,'* or when she would go to school and graduate from college. He wouldn't be there when she got married, to hand her over to that man who would cherish her forever. He wasn't going to be there for any of that.

Tears flowed down Tommie's face. He was going to end the pain and get to rest finally. His life had been a journey; he was grateful, though. It was a lesson and a blessing.

Everything went quiet and dark; it was cold. He felt still, and calmness washed over him. He smiled to himself as he took the last heave of relief. It was over!

Grace and Dorothy returned to find Tommie sunken in the bathroom tub. He drowned himself after he took a bottle of Oxycodone. Tommie's body was wrinkled and white. Dorothy yelled, "Oh no! We were only gone for a few hours!" Dorothy immediately called EMS. By the time they arrived and tried to revive him, Tommie was gone.

Charlie got the news from Dorothy and rushed home. "No, not my Tommie!" She laid there on the ground in the bathroom next to the tub. She took his hand and prayed.

The louder she prayed, the more she cried. The was the part of life she did not want to face. Why could I not save my husband? Did the visit from Sidney really push him the over the edge? Why was her presence so deadly to him? So many unanswered questions.

As the coroner left with his body, Charlie did not say a word. She simply walked away, grabbed Grace, and went to her room. Charlie stayed in bed for a few days; she wasn't eating and was barely tending to Grace. Her mom and Mrs. Dempsey were there day and night, fearful that Charlie would fall into a deep depressive state.

Charlie had to make funeral arrangements for the husband, her best friend, and confidant. She cried out, "How can I do this alone? Why did he leave Grace and me? WHY???"

Charlie and Tommie's sister planned the funeral arrangements, a quiet celebration of life with friends and family. Tommie and Grace kept their circle small. They did not have too many friends. His friends from college who were in the accident with him survived and had no idea they would attend his funeral. Charlie was surrounded by family and friends, but she looked pale, as if she wasn't really there. She tried to hold herself together, but there were so many thoughts in her head.

Charlie took a leave of absence from work to gather herself. She needed a plan for her life. She didn't expect to live life without Tommie. Charlie asked Tommie's college friends to meet with her; she needed answers. It had to be more than what he told her. He survived the attack from the car accident, yet he could not survive a visit from Sidney?

Charlie had to get a grasp on life. She did not want Grace to endure life as her mother did. She wanted to be a strong mother to her daughter. Charlie arranged for Tommie's friends to come over to talk to her. Hoping she would get the answers she was searching for.

Before their arrival, Charlie found a letter from Tommie sitting on top of the fireplace next to her blue vase. It was the place where they would sit and talk. They had their best conversations by the fireplace, so of course, that is where he would leave the letter. He also knew the vase would be where she would find answers and mend the cracks in her heart.

My dearest Charlie,

I want to apologize for leaving this way. I want you to know that I love you with all my heart and every bit of my soul. Please let Grace know that my living was not in vain. She will be perfect in the eyes of you and God. Love her unconditionally, and give her the best of you. I never wanted things to end this way.

From the first day we met, I knew I wanted to marry you; your gentle sweet spirit was what I needed and wanted in a life partner. You provided me with encouragement and comfort. I wanted to be your friend and your lover, but I humbly accepted to take things slow. If I could have married you on the spot, I would've. It was you that I wanted to be a better person for, it was you that made counseling a way of life. If it weren't for you, my dead soul might have disintegrated sooner. I must confess I wasn't true to you in the beginning.

Let me start by saying I never wanted to hurt you; you were the angel I needed. I knew if I told you who I was really was, you would've left me. Yes, I am Thomas Whittaker, and yes, I have a gang of siblings from my mom and dad and my dad's extra family. What I didn't share with you or anyone except Sidney is the day my life changed forever. My parents were arguing as usual. My dad's girlfriend and my mom were arguing about his other kids when the woman came over with the kids in tow. They were all there in my house with my family.

It was time for me to react. I grabbed my mom's arm to remove her from the heated argument. The mistress was in my father's face, waving a gun and pleading with my dad to leave his real family behind. As I approached my dad's mistress to protect my mom, I managed to get the gun from her. When I pulled away, the gun went off, shooting my dad. I shot my father.

Shocked, I thought maybe I did this on purpose. Could I commit such a heinous crime? My mom and the other woman were screaming, the kids were running everywhere, and I stood there frozen, as if time stood still. When the ambulance and police arrived, they said my father was shot in the shoulder and neck. I had no idea I shot him twice; I blanked out, I guess from rage.

We weren't sure if my dad was going to live. He was rushed to the hospital, and my mom went with him. The police stayed to question everyone. Without hesitation, his mistress told the police I shot my dad. I was taken into custody for attempted murder. I was 14 years old at the time. My mom came to my aide. She explained the accident and that it was not intentional. At the hospital, Dad spent several hours in surgery and survived. Honestly, I was bitter he survived yet relieved. The hell he gave my mom would've stopped if he died, and I would've gladly spent the rest of my life in prison for my mom. My dad was never the same after the surgery, yet he did not file charges, and I was released. My mom always says it was her fault my dad was with other women; that's why he treated her so poorly. She even stayed with him after all that happened. I distanced myself from the family and my father. My mom wasn't the same after that either. Even though my dad was around, he wasn't present. He was drunk most of the time, but my mom stood up for him. Deep down inside, I resented her and hated him. He was a coward and a punk; he did not uphold his duties as a father and a husband.

I never told anyone that I resented my mother, I always showed her decency and respect. I vowed to always be there for her. I never had a relationship with my dad after that. In college, I met Sidney shortly after all of the chaos simmered down. She carried me through nights of tears and fears but cheated with several men. I never trusted women after that. And then I met you, and you gave me life. But when Sidney showed up, all those old wounds opened back up. I can't deal with the pain and guilt anymore, so goodbye is the only way I know to stop the pain.

My love, I am sorry, but this is the only way; believe me: my heart will still be with you. The house is paid for, and all accounts are in your name with a hefty insurance policy. I know finances can never make up for losing me like this, but I want to keep my promise to provide for you and Grace. I will always love you.

Charlie sat in awe for a moment before the men arrived. She had the answers she needed. When Tommie's friends arrived, she showed them the letter he left. They all sat there with their jaws dropped to the floor. They did not know Tommie was going through anything, they only knew he kept himself together. Tommie was walking around holding his world on his shoulders, and no one knew. Charlie now needed to move on with her life, broken and shattered, without her Tommie.

Reminiscing

Charlie enjoyed their company for a few hours until she was ready to put Grace down for bed. While contemplating a new direction for her life, her phone rang. It was Nikki on the other end. She hung up immediately, she wasn't ready to deal with Nikki. Charlie grabbed a picture of Tommie and talked to it. "Why weren't you honest with me? We could've faced this together."

The first thing on her list was to go to therapy the next day. Charlie went into detail with her therapist and showed her the letter. The therapist explained people of trauma oftentimes never heal. They go through life with hopes of self-healing. Even worse, friends can see odd behavior. They rather talk about you rather than help you. She wanted Charlie to know this was not her fault.

Tommie was one of many Black men who are trodden down with life and scared to get help or admit they need a refuge of safety. There are many like Tommie who can't admit their journey is guided by false misrepresentation. She encouraged Charlie to go forward in life and, most importantly, to be there for Grace. She will need a strong person so she doesn't go through life like her mom and dad. Charlie mentioned that she heard from Nikki. The therapist advised Charlie to close that old wound.

On the ride home, she dialed the number that Nikki called her from. Nikki answered, but the silence was evidence they needed closure. Nikki offered her condolences to Charlie, which started the conversation. Nikki went back to the day of Charlie's rape, she admitted leaving her on purpose.

"I didn't know how to be there for you at the time. All I could do was walk away. That was the hardest decision I made in my life; life was never the same from then on. I blamed myself, but Charlie, I never meant to hurt you. I know what hurt really is. There was torture every day, and I ran on an empty stomach most days. Some days I was left alone in the basement without water and lights. I will admit I saw a friend in you, but I also saw someone I could control. I enjoyed our friendship because you were vulnerable. I couldn't control my home life, so it was easy to control you. You would do anything for me, and I used that against you. I cherished our friendship yet carried a deep hurt inside of me. Yes, I abandoned you. I was never saved, so I couldn't save you, didn't even know how to. The saying that goes, 'hurt people hurt other people is true,' I know I hurt you. Please forgive me, this isn't an easy conversation, and I am sure Sidney told you I was in prison for attempted murder. After many nights of running the streets from coast to coast, I ran into Dwight. I befriended him so I could set him up, and I stabbed him 10 times; he is now paralyzed from my actions. That may not have been the best decision; however, I wanted him to suffer for what he did to you. In actuality, I was suffering for what I did to you too. So, I am here serving a life sentence for almost killing Dwight, your rapist."

"You didn't attempt to kill him for me. You did it out of guilt. From your conversation, you NEVER were a friend to me. I was someone you preyed on. I trusted you with my life, but you left me helpless and afraid. You deserve to be where you are, and I hope you will never call me back. Nikki, I trusted you. I can understand how you were hurting because I was hurting as well from similar abuse. However, no matter what we didn't discuss, I would've never left you like a stray animal. I cared for you as a friend and sister, Nikki. I know life hasn't been easy or fair for either of us, but the decisions I made were based on the hurt I endured. There were plenty of times where I wanted to kill or destroy that person who killed my spirit and joy. I chose to help myself by getting the help I needed to move forward. I can only hope you are seeing someone in prison to get the help you need. I forgive you, Nikki, not for you but for myself. I ask that you never contact me again; my peace requires me to move on from you. Goodbye!"

Charlie dropped the phone and sat on the floor in a sea of pictures from her childhood and a journal of the days of she and Nikki spent together. She was trying to piece together that time in life; instead of putting the puzzle pieces together, she laid there and cried the night away.

Dorothy and Grace were downstairs; her mom didn't know Charlie was going to another place in her mind. The following day, Charlie's mom found her on the floor in the same spot from the previous night, in the middle of a puzzle, the puzzle of life. Charlie didn't know her mom was there; her mom began to read the journals from Charlie's past and started to shed tears. Dorothy thought of what she had done to her daughter. She caused lifelong pain her innocent daughter wasn't prepared for. She thought running away from her responsibilities would make them go away. The hurt and neglect she faced as a kid made her turn her back on her daughter. Her issues caused her to become a broken vessel. She never knew her distorted life would damage her child, the child she never wanted. She abandoned her without the presence and love. Charlie reminded Dorothy of her father, whom she hated with all her being. She was a reminder of him leaving her with a child she never wanted. "Charlie was born without hope for a future and a life I couldn't give her."

Dorothy regretted her actions, she looked at her daughter on the floor as she continued to weep. Charlie sat up and turned to her mother. She understood her mother now, reasons why she left her alone all by herself, although she would never do that to Grace. They hugged for a while.

Dorothy felt peace within her, the one she had never felt in her life. Things were going to be better, and she knew it. She was going to be strong for her daughter and granddaughter.

The Dawn of a New Day

Charlie gathered herself together finally to go to work. They did not say much after they held each other. Charlie prepared breakfast and got Grace ready for the day. Her mom was the live-in babysitter and support system. They were set to go on with life as normal as possible.

Charlie began to ponder a new way to heal that would to help other women of all ages to heal from cracked vessels. She began to draft a letter to the shelter director she and Tommie volunteered with who was a good friend of Mrs. Dempsey.

"I am Charlie, lost and confused about life, yet I have a story to tell, and I am healing every day. I have a story to tell other women who can heal from a broken past. I recently lost my husband to suicide because he battled things he never recovered from and refused to talk about. It was him that made me realize to be free and break the chains that were holding me back for so many years, understanding guilt and repressed memories can trigger more hurt. I can honestly say I know that I will find peace. Peace of mind is the best gift I can give to myself and other women. It took 30 plus years to know I could control my destiny with God's guidance. If I hold on to the past, my future can never be bright and full of joy. I would like to open up 'Charlie's Closet,' where women can undress their wounds, unpack their baggage, freely expose themselves, opening dialogue without fear and judgment. With your approval, I would be delighted to share my journey to give women hope and the dawn of a new day."

Charlie left work to go home; she stopped by the shelter to give her letter to the director. As she was walking out the door, the director yelled, "Come back. I am a quick reader. I would love for you to share your story with others." Charlie replied, "It is at the shelter where I found a passion, a passion to help and inspire women to be vessels, not victims."

Charlie left the shelter with a new mindset, an idea to keep Tommie's legacy alive. Charlie's Closet would be a safe space for women to vent, release and exhale, where women could heal one another. The therapist agreed to help Charlie and provide counseling.

The room was decorated with bright blue pillows and plush lounging chairs. The walls were popping with vibrant purple tones. The carpet was soft and cozy for them to sit on the floor and share. You could even grab a blanket for security. Her therapist placed books on healing on the shelves in the center. On the shelf was Charlie's blue vase, with ashes from Tommie's body. It was a symbol of restoration for Charlie and the women who came to the closet.

Dorothy and Mrs. Dempsey were a big help with meals and finding housing for the women and their kids. Charlie was living her life and dreaming of bigger opportunities. Grace was growing and becoming the young girl she envisioned for herself.

Six months have gone by, and Charlie was working, volunteering, and Charlie's Closet was in full swing.

"Now, ladies, that's the story of my life," she smiled at them as she crossed her legs

"Wow, Mrs. Whitaker, that's a lot that happened to you," a fifteen-year-old girl said to her.

"Yes, it was a lot, but I am much better now. Does anybody have any questions?"

"How do you feel now after everything that has happened?" another kid asked.

"Well, I feel better and more fulfilled because I have something to keep me going. I am not going to give up for anything. Even when it gets hard, I am going to continue."

"How do you plan on doing that?"

"I am going to love myself first because that is the first important thing to learn before anything else. When you love yourself, you will be able to accept yourself and grow. Although it's going to be tough, you know that there is a reward for you in the end." She paused. "I have a baby girl that I want to guide to become a better person, so I have to be a better person first before I say I want to guide anyone else. My daughter and lot of other people look up to me."

"But Mrs. Whitaker, why didn't you get back with your friend when she called? Like maybe give her a call or visit her in prison," a brown-haired kid stood up and asked her.

Charlie smiled and took her time to reply to him. "Connor, you see, there are some people you will meet in life who will either shape or destroy your vessel. Those kinds of people are unavoidable, but it depends on you to filter out who molds and who breaks. Nikki was my friend who I thought was molding my vessel, but she was actually destroying it. Luckily, I got out of that friendship, but I cannot go back again…."

"Why Mrs. Whitaker?" a five-year-old girl interrupted.

"Because the time we spent as friends is over. It's time for me to move forward and mold my healed vessel with the right people."

Charlie enjoyed being with the children. Teaching them to learn to accept themselves and love who they were.

"You are a vessel brought into this world and created by God. The kind of people you move with can determine how your vessel will be. Actually, I'll say it's the people you allow into your life. Growing up, I had no friends, and I wasn't shown love even by a single bit by any of my family members. So, the friend I managed to trust them with everything I had, which was my little fragile and vulnerable heart. A lot of people took advantage of me, causing my vessel to break even more. But later, I met with the right people who began to help me shape it. Like Mrs. Dempsey and her husband, Miranda, and my dearest husband, Tommie," Charlie wiped the tear from her eye and continued.

"These people helped in molding my me. I was hesitant and reluctant at first because I had been hurt by so many people in my life. Still, these people never gave up on me, and I am grateful to them for the love and care they have shown me. So, I tell you today, kids, love yourself, appreciate yourself. You may have come from broken homes, and some of you might have not but never ever let anyone belittle you. An old friend once told me that she would never allow anybody to belittle her. I was amazed at first, I thought she was going to beat them up, but she told me she was going to accept herself first. It is only when you don't love and accept yourself that people find it as an opportunity to dominate you. Be humble not stupid. Protect your vessel well, and be happy always. You are in charge of your happiness."

"Ohhhh," the kids were amazed.

"Mrs. Whitaker," a Black boy stood up, "How do you want to live the rest of your life now?"

"I want to… live it Happily, with no regrets whatsoever."

Charlie answered a few more questions before the kids went to their homes. She was healing and would continue to heal. She was in charge of her happiness now and would live every bit of it every day.

She left the shelter one night, and on her way home, she had a moment of despair. Everything was going well, so what was wrong? She looked on her phone again, and there was Malik's number, the ghost of the past, her first heartbreak. Why was he calling, and why now? Life is fantastic!

Charlie made her way home and listened to the voicemail. He wanted to talk about the past and possibly the future. She laid Grace down for the night and called Malik back.

Malik was ready to go full throttle on what happened when he left a year many years ago. Malik began to explain to Charlie that life for him wasn't the same after they separated.

"I hurt you for my selfishness of wanting more which turned out to the worse mistake of my life. I ask for your forgiveness and the possibility of starting over."

Malik married the woman that he left Charlie for, but they had no children. Ironically, she cheated on him and had a child from another man and tried to pin the child on him. Charlie said to Malik, "That's your karma that played on your life. You left me alone and destitute. Now you expect me to forget the wrong you did and move on as if nothing happened. That is ridiculous! You haven't asked what's going on with me, assuming I'm alone, well, I am not. I have a gorgeous little girl who is my whole world! My husband committed suicide, and my mom and I live together. Life hasn't been easy or fair. I can forgive, but I can never forget what you did to me. I can't hate you anymore, but I can't love you and pretend you never broke me down either."

"Well, can we at least be friends? Honestly, Charlie, you were the best thing that ever happened to me. I was young and dumb. I wasn't ready to give what you needed. I'm begging for you to be in my life as a friend. I'd love to meet Grace one day. I hope you'll trust me again. I feel in my heart we were meant to be together. The first true love of my life. I haven't felt the same with any woman as I felt with you. You don't have to answer now. Just think on it, I will be in touch, and Charlie... I love you."

Charlie was in disbelief again, another call from the past. Why did her past keep coming up, first Nikki now this fool? And the nerve of him to say he loved her; the boy must be losing his mind. The past needs to stay in the past. Maybe it was a test to see how strong she would be and not allow them to dictate her future.

Charlie wasn't going to let any of them send her to a dark place anymore. She held her head to the sky. The room was dark, and the storms were raging in her thoughts. Charlie needed to let go of the past and move towards the future for Grace. Grace needed to see what a healthy and peaceful life looked like. Her little daughter was not going to be a victim of her own past and brokenness. She was going to be loved and nurtured to be a bright young woman.

Her mother made mistakes, she neglected her, made several the wrong decisions. Though she wasn't perfect, she was healing. Charlie promised she was going to be there for her daughter.

Thankfully, the broken vessels were healing. By no means would Charlie abandon Grace or make her feel inferior.

"Grace is what I am living for; her life depends on my happiness."

Charlie did forgive Malik, and they began talking regularly as friends. He understood her new journey, and he was in love with Charlie for the second time in his life.

Charlie drifted off to sleep to the howling wind. She dreamed of the new days ahead. Life could not get better. Charlie was on her own after many years of fears and tears. Nothing could interrupt the new Charlie. She was going to be strong now and even stronger for her child, but most important of all for Tommie in heaven who was watching her.

She felt the cool breeze blow on her face. He was there with her, cheering her on in the new journey. It was a new dawn, time for the vessel to rise.

About the Author

Tosha Suggs is a proud mother of one, yet mothers many youths. I am excited to have been a vessel to so many young people.

I recall as a child, I put myself to sleep at night thinking about a story to write, a story to tell. Thinking one day those stories would be a vision to write a book.

It was 2017 when I got the notion, but not the nudge to pursue my dream of becoming an author. In 2017, I lost my mother and my best friend within 6 months of each other, which truly a devastating impact on my life. That part of life took me into a dark and gloomy phase where I thought there was no end to the suffering. However, with prayer and patience. I picked myself up and dreamed of endless possibilities for myself. After two long years, I put pen to paper and started to write using a pile of old journals and my thoughts.

As I began the journey, I realized so many people are broken vessels, whether by circumstances or tragedies in their lives. I want this book to help you heal and stop hiding behind a mask of what people think you should be or feel.

My prayer is to never let your broken vessel make you a victim.

Made in the USA
Columbia, SC
13 March 2022